W
g

Look for the continuing
adventures of
Santa and Margaret
in
Santa's Greatest Pursuit
available in 2009

Santa's
Second
Chance

Irene Zulueta

Santa's Second Chance
Irene Zulueta

Winlock Publishing co.
26135 Murrieta rd
Sun city Ca 92585
(951) 943-0014
www.winlockgaley.com

Associate editor Hal Lingerman

ISBN 1-890461-49-0

Price $14.95

ORDER BLANK

For additional copies of the following books send check
or money order to:

ECHOED VISIONS
P.O. BOX 97
SUN CITY, CA 92586-3757

—— Christmas Fantasy ⁣ @ $11.95 ——

—— Santa's In-Between Years ⁣ @ $14.95 ——

—— Santa's **Second Chance** ⁣ @ $14.95 ——

Shipping & handling ⁣ $4.00

Total ⁣ ——————

Name _____

Address _____

City, St, Zip _____

(No Credit Cards Please)

Wishing

Wishing's a game not only children play,
Wishing's a game for now and everyday!
Wishing can make your wildest dreams come
true,
Dreams that you dreamt were never meant
for you, so . . .

Wish, wish your heart away,
Look, look for a brighter day.
Dream, dreams that are here to stay,
Whatever you fathom, come what may, so . . .
Wish, wish your heart away,
Look for a brighter day,
Dream, dreams they're here to stay
Fathom let come what may, for . . .
Wishing's a game not only children play,
Wishing's a game for now and everyday.
Wishing can make your wildest dreams come true,
Wishing's just for you!

Irene Pichlik Zulueta

Contents

Irene Zulueta

STARTING OVER

Several years had passed and to all appearances, out of nowhere, Santa began reliving his dreams.

Majoring the art of being able to fly their very own team of reindeer, Fred and Donald had been back and forth to Ireland with their wives several times in the process of transferring the children to their prospective schools.

Coming home in the summer and on holidays, the children would participate in the gymnastics they had grown to love, along with Rex, who continued as their instructor.

Outside of learning to maneuver the flight of reindeer and taking the trips to Ireland, in spite of holding a 49% partnership, Fred and Donald, did nothing to enhance or promote the business.

Being aware of this fact, Santa did not complain because this was his project and he really wanted to do things his way. He was afraid they would come up with ideas he'd rather not comply with; so he said nothing until the day he began imagining his dream, once again coming alive.

One day, as Santa and Alex played WORDFORM, he decided to give Alex a preview of his imagination, knowing he might help with suggestions enabling him to continue the ideas he dreamt of before he became to sick to go on.

"Alex," Santa said, "I'm beginning to get bored with all of this sitting around, playing games and having not much else to do except eat, walk the pets, play some more games, go to sleep, get up in the morning . . .can you see where I'm coming from?"

Surprisingly, Alex offered Santa an answer. "Precisely, you want to continue with SANTA KLAUS ANONYMOUS, but do you feel up to it?"

Pondering his question Santa responded, "Alex, I feel fine; Margaret has me on a substantial diet, and I don't like the idea of just wasting away with nothing but time to spare.

We have all the manpower we need, you have built all of the buildings we had planned to use, and if we don't use them, they will go to waste; we have toys galore waiting to be delivered, but we have no one to take orders for them. How could everything go so wrong?"

Responding to Santa's thoughts, Alex said, "Santa, maybe you just needed a phase of time out. If you feel up to it, then let's start over, but a little slower.

Why don't we call a meeting and see what the others think? Maybe they are as tired of doing nothing as you have been."

"Well said," answered Santa, "is tomorrow too soon for this meeting?"

Having his usual enthusiasm Alex replied, "I'm certain, once I get the word out among those involved, the question asked will be, why didn't we do it yesterday?"

"Terrific," Santa continued, "if you will spread the news, I'll discuss it with Margaret."

So Alex went on his way and Santa looked for Margaret in the kitchen where he knew he'd find her; this was her day to bake cookies.

Entering the kitchen, Santa called, "Margaret, I've got great news!"

Santa's Second Chance

Inquiring what it might be, she sat down at the table and patiently waited for Santa to begin his explanation.

"Hon," Santa began, "You know, I feel as if I'm wasting away in my old age; I need more action. I've been thinking, well . . ." he stammered and hesitated waiting for her to object, but she offered no comment and went on listening as Santa spoke softly, slowly and purposefully. "You see Hon, once I had a dream and when I grew ill, my thoughts turned to negativity; but really, I'm tired of sitting around, playing games... I want to revive Santa Klaus Anonymous. Do you have any objections if I restart that which I discontinued?"

Answering his question, Margaret told him, "Your wish Dear, is my desire. Knowing how hard you worked, if you decide to retract your efforts, it's all-right with me, as long as you do it sensibly; that is so you don't have another seizure; you know how much I love you and . . ."

Finishing what he thought she was trying to say, Santa concluded, "And Margaret, I know how hard it was for you when I became ill . . . and I promise if ever I begin to feel a weakness coming on . . ."

Ending his sentence Margaret specified, "I hope you will find me immediately."

"By all means," answered Santa as he asked, "Sweetheart, do you think we should start over?"

Without an ounce of hesitancy, Margaret agreed.

"Good," answered Santa. "We are calling a meeting for tomorrow; will you deliver the message to Fred and Donald for me?"

"Hon," she replied, "I don't mind delivering messages, but

I think you should try to develop a little more camaraderie with the O'Hares and Gilpatricks by going up there yourself so they don't think you have grown weary of them."

"I suppose you are right," responded Santa, "but just this once will you do it for me?"

Her answer was "Yes I will, but next time, at least come with me."

To her surprise, Santa said, "Margaret, why don't we go up there right now. I have nothing better to do."

Being pleased with Santa's willingness, she said, "I'm ready, let's go." and out the door they went to pay a congenial visit to the Gilpatricks and the O'Hares.

Answering the door, Fred was surprised to find Santa and Margaret.

"Come in guys . . ., and welcome to our humble abode," exclaimed Fred. Inviting them to sit down in the parlor, Dorothy offered them something to drink.

Speaking first as he was certain Margaret would want him to do Santa asked, "is Donald anywhere around?"

Telling him he had just stepped out to check on the reindeer, Fred describing Donald's behavior explained, "You know, when Patrick is away at school, Donald goes down to the barn everyday to be assured they are safe and sound. I'm not certain who is fondest of these animals, Donald or Patrick, and he should return shortly."

Trying to strike up a conversation, Santa went on to tell Fred, "You undoubtedly know, old age is for the birds, but since I'm not a bird, I have decided not to give in to it; old age that is.

Santa's Second Chance

Feeling better since my heart has shaped up, I have decided to restart the business I once dreamt of having by simply starting over; on the same track of course, but with fresh ideas in mind.

We have a post office, a weather tower, a workshop and a barn big enough to hold all the animals.

Consequently, I'm here today to tell you I'm calling a meeting for tomorrow. Since you and Donald are both partners, I'd like to see you there, but this time, we will hold the meeting in the Conference Room at the post office; it's time to pick up where we left off."

Being utterly surprised, Fred felt totally enthused about the prospect of returning to business. In his mind it meant if things returned to normal along with profits, there would be bonuses. That possibility would not only enable him to enjoy a better life style, it would also allow him to be able to support his children's higher education when it became a necessity.

Knowing Donald and Mary would also be enthused once he told them of the projects reinvention, he could hardly wait to pass on the news.

Dorothy, sitting alongside of Margaret seemed to be fascinated by Santa's revelation. Having to say something, she did telling her, "You know, I too am getting bored. Not having the children home, I've found myself reminiscing about the business we were going to start; you had so many ideas, and all this time has passed. Now we have nothing when we could have been so productive; maybe it's not too late to rethink those ideas and start up again."

Though it was definitely a step in the right direction, Margaret was hardly able to believe what she had just heard and asked, "Tell me Dorothy, how does Mary feel about starting over?"

"It's funny you should ask," replied Dorothy, "we were just talking about this very subject the other day. I'll bet she would be happy to pick up where we left off."

Since Donald had not returned, Santa suggested that Fred relay the message to him and that he also mention attending the meeting tomorrow at one o'clock sharp in the Conference Room."

"We too will have our own meeting if you'd like," Margaret told Dorothy, "I'm just not certain when, but I will let you know."

Looking at the clock, Margaret told Santa it was almost dinner time so they had better be on their way."

Agreeing with her Santa expelled his thoughts to Fred telling him "It's been great having this conversation with you Fred; now don't forget to tell Donald about the meeting and I'll see both of you tomorrow."

Being anxious to compare notes, Margaret and Santa left the Gilpatricks hurriedly and rushed back to their own apartment. On the other hand, Fred could hardly wait to tell Donald what had occurred, so he told Dorothy, "I have to find Donald; I can't wait to deliver the news."

Knowing his concern for Santa, Fred added, "I just hope Santa is well enough for this undertaking, you know he isn't getting any younger."

Reassuring Fred, Dorothy informed him, "You know Margaret takes good care of Santa and she wouldn't encourage this plan of action if she didn't think he was up to it."

Later, in the Klaus residence after finishing dinner, Margaret and Santa walked Mewpurr and Snapper while discussing the events of the day.

That night, they both went to bed with smiles on their faces, the same way they awoke in the morning, ready to think of . . . .

STARTING OVER! ! !

NEW ENDEAVORS

When Santa and Margaret awoke, one might think they were wearing face masks as their smiles were totally fixed.

As Santa opened his eyes, the first thing he said was, "Praise the Lord, I'm alive, well, and this is the first day of the rest of my life."

Casting a glance at Santa, Margaret smiled, and timidly said, "Me too!"

They dressed, had breakfast and Santa bid farewell to Margaret as he practically ran to his office. Sitting at his desk he started making a list of all the projects he wanted to discuss with those attending the meeting.

First, he would ask each chief if they still had the desire to pickup where they left off several years ago. Then he would ask them where and if any, working conditions needed to be improved. Next he would inquire if they found their living conditions comfortable as Alfred, Alfonso, and Alex had already moved into their quarters in the post office.

Having moved to Ireland into the house with Mildred, to help with the children if need be, Leon, Phillip, and Nancy would not be attending the meeting. Actually, this arrangement worked out quite satisfactorily.

The children were happy about returning to school in Ireland, and Patrick was permitted to take two of the kittens, Rascal and Tyrant with him. It was clear that if funds were available to educate him as a veterinarian, having become such a huge animal fan, it would come to be a part of his 'DESTINY'.

Realizing he had gone off on an irrelevant line of projection, Santa looked at his pad of paper and saw only three topics for discussion; and there were so many more subjects to consider he decided to summon Alex for help. Leaving his office, Santa headed for the workshop where he thought Alex could be found.

Upon entering the workshop, he saw Jeffry sweeping the floor, but Alex was nowhere around. Santa asked Russell, who was busy writing specifications for a toy ship he was contemplating building, where he might find him.

"You know," responded Russell, "it's hard to keep up with that guy. One minute you see him, then you don't. He moves like the wind and yet, he's always here when you need him."

Not seeing Alex, Santa asked, "If that's the case, where is he?"

"Well sir, if you will look toward the door," answered Russell, "I do believe that is Alex coming through it right now."

Looking in the recommended direction, he saw Alex hurrying toward them. Calling directly to Santa he told him, "I've been to your place and you weren't there so my next guess was, you'd come looking for me in the workshop."

Though feeling a bit confused, Santa had no problem asking Alex to return with him to his office where they could talk freely.

"By all means!" responded Alex and the two of them found their way back as Santa anxiously asked, "Were you able to get in touch with everyone who should be attending the meeting?"

Replying "They will all be there with bells on," Santa questioned Alex's interpretation of 'being there with bells on'. Knowing he didn't understand that expression, Alex told Santa, "they will be there, and can hardly wait to resume the original plan."

Accepting Alex's explanation, Santa showed him the list of questions he had written which he hoped would inspire everyone to come up with ideas.

Looking at the short list Santa had compiled, Alex told him, "I can understand your concern for the answer to these questions, but they don't suggest a proposal that will address the solution. They will love you all the more because you are showing deep concern for their welfare, but their well-being is not the solution for which you are looking.

First at hand, we should ask if anyone has any serious ideas about a name for the business; at this time let's just take notes and we can go over them later.

Then we have the question of advertising for Santa Klaus Anonymous!

Furthermore, we need someone with the capabilities of directing a Santa Klaus Anonymous Class. Where will it be held . . . how will we advertise . . . where will the men apply for an interview . . . when they arrive, will they stay over for several days, or will we have to shuttle them right back to where they came from! Where will they get their suits, you know . . . like the one Margaret made for you? Are they going to get paid or do we expect them to be volunteer workers?" Hearing what Santa thought were Alex's critical remarks, he suddenly thought, have I bit off more than I can chew! Then he asked himself, "Am I developing a negative attitude again?" Answering his own question, the voice in his mind was shouting loud and clear saying, "No! You can do this; the problem is, you've been lying dormant for too long; you need to get with it!"

Looking at the clock he realized he hadn't finished his list; it had to be completed in the next hour before anyone arrived.

Hearing a knock on the door, Santa asked Alex to answer it. In doing so, he found Dolores and Margaret, each holding a tray filled with luncheon snacks, waiting to enter the room.

Margaret told Santa, "When you didn't come home for lunch, I knew you'd be hungry, so I fixed two trays of snacks for you and your friends. Dolores and I will be back with punch and lemonade to help with thirsty appetites."

Having already left the office Santa remembered, he hadn't called for the meeting in his office, he had recommended it be held in the Conference Room of the post office.

Now he not only had qualifying projects to worry about, but he also needed to find a way of moving the food to the Conference Room. Bellowing loudly, Santa called, "Alex . . . help!"

Jokingly, Alex said to him, "Santa, I have no magical powers, but I think if you will wait for Margaret and Dolores to return, we can ask them to help us move the trays to the Conference Room where the meeting is going to be held."

Immediately apologizing to Alex, and knowing he had jumped the gun, Santa asked, "Am I getting too old for this game?"

Delivering a most apropos answer, Alex responded, "No Santa, you just aren't in practice. Why, in no time at all, you'll be back in action, wondering why everyone is so far behind. Cheer up, this is all part of the game we call, 'Love It or Leave It', and we know your choice don't we?"

Returning with pitchers of drinks for everyone, Santa again apologized, telling Margaret and Dolores they had caught him off guard. While explaining how he told Fred the meeting was to be held in the Conference Room," he said, "I'm sorry, as you were talking to Dorothy, you probably didn't hear me, and I forgot to make a point of mentioning it to you."

Accepting Santa's apology, Margaret said, "No problem. We will just move everything if you and Alex will help."

"Of course," answered Alex, and Santa offered his, "Thank you."

Moving all of the food to the Conference Room where everyone was waiting for the meeting to convene, Santa noticed he left his comments behind and had also forgotten what he had written on his paper; he hoped Alex brought along copies of his notes.

Before starting the meeting, Santa invited everyone to partake in the snacks; afterwards they would proceed with their discussions.

Addressing the audience he began by saying, "I'm glad to see you all made an effort to find your way to this meeting so we can continue to acknowledge what we all made such an earnest attempt to develop, a subject close to my heart, none other than 'SANTA KLAUS ANONYMOUS'. I've had thoughts about several subjects which I would like to discuss, and then I will ask Alex to take over.

"First of all," Santa asked, "is there anyone here who does not wish to continue the appointment to which they have been promoted? If you are in favor of your appointments raise your hand, say 'AYE' and we will go on to the next subject." Happy to see all the hands and voices he heard, Santa then asked, "About your living conditions, are there any problems?"

As the room grew silent, they looked at one another and he continued, "The fact that you are all content with your quarters makes me happy, and last but not least, are there any questions regarding your working conditions?"

Raising his hand Santa inquired, "Yes, is there a problem Alex?"

He explained to Santa, that the quantity of toys continuing to accumulate have outgrown the size of the workshop. We either need to build a larger workshop where we can store the over abundance or find someplace to which they can be transferred.

Picturing a showroom Santa replied, "Alex, you know, I hate to ask you to put up another building, so why don't we take a look at the castle; there are so many rooms available, especially on the first floor. Perhaps we could turn a few of them into storage areas and others into showrooms. A thorough inspection will address this problem and we should do this as soon as we are able.

If there are no other questions," Santa went on, "I will turn this meeting over to Alex, our Chief of Operations."

Not having heard Santa earlier, he hadn't realized he was going to ask him to conduct any part of this discussion, but as usual, Alex was glad to help in any way he could.

"Well," he began, "there are several subjects we have to address. One of them is a name; to be more accurate, a business name. If you will put on your thinking caps, maybe we can come up with an appropriate name by the next meeting. Finding a new name for Santa's business for the most part is the purpose of this meeting.

We are also going to need another secretary at this location. Since Nancy is working in Ireland with Leon and Phillip, we will need one to handle our affairs here in Santa Land. I know of three or four possibilities, but I believe our best choice would be Vivian; her experience is quite extensive and if there are no other suggestions, we can go on to the next subject.

We need a teacher for the Santa class and I believe Joseph, who was a teacher, would be the best one for the job, size-wise as well as, knowledge-wise."

Asking Fred and Donald how many helpers they thought they would need, not only to work with, but to accompany them on their trips to Ireland . . . he told them this figure could be reported at the next meeting, since there was quite a bit of work to be done before the post office became operational.

Moving right along, Alex approached the subject of an interviewer for the men answering the advertisement that would say, 'SANTAS WANTED'. He told them, " I think this category falls into Santa's territory because, while we were going to teach them in Santa Land, it might be better to hold classes in Ireland until we have an idea of how we can adjust, and also, to see how many applications we receive. Leon and Phillip are in Ireland working on the advertising, or I should say, will be, once we give them the okay to go ahead.

For now, unless someone has more questions or topics for discussion, we will adjourn this meeting until next week."

Adding a final statement before the group cleared the Conference Room Alex announced, "Remember guys, put on your thinking caps and let's find a name for 'Santa Klaus Anonymous'. We may even offer a prize to the person who comes up with the most original or best name."

Being awestruck at this suggestion, Santa thought why not? A little competition and activity in this village certainly couldn't hurt the morale any.

Calling out to Fred and Donald, Santa asked if they would stay as he wanted to talk to them. He also requested Alex take notes so he could schedule whatever they proposed.

Thinking ahead, Santa asked them when they were going to make their next trip to Ireland. Answering him, Fred replied, "The children will soon be out of school for spring vacation, and that is when we were planning to make the next trip."

Responding Santa said "We may have to make a trip before then so we can let Phillip and Leon in on the latest activity. It won't happen before our next meeting, but for now, at least I know what and how to plan. At any rate, I'll see you at the next meeting, if I don't see you sooner!"

Fred and Donald knew this was their signal to exit, and they hurried home to relay the news to Dorothy and Mary.

Feeling it was time for his afternoon nap, Santa and Alex walked back to his office to find his favorite, overstuffed chair, waiting to provide him with the comfort to which he'd grown accustomed. As he set his head back on the pillow, Alex departed, leaving Santa content, asleep and dancing himself into Dreamland, devouring any dreams he could find involving . . . . . .

New Endeavors

Irene Zulueta

MEANT TO BE

Later in the day, as Santa napped, Margaret and Dolores picked up the leftover mess. Having yet to decide when she would hold her meeting with Dorothy and Mary, Margaret thought of how she had actually discarded the idea of going into business when Santa became ill.

Thinking the situation over, Margaret knew she too had a list to make of workable subjects. Realizing that after a few years these matters were not idly dwelling in her head waiting to be discussed, she decided to do it immediately.

Sitting at the table in the kitchen with paper and pencil in hand, Margaret reminded herself, after looking at the clock, she would soon have to start preparing dinner.

The first topic on her list was going to be the R-T-R-T (ARTY-ARTY) scratching posts, a sample of which she had already produced. Next would be the cat and dog beds waiting to be sewn, as the stuffed animals were already in production; and how about a cook book, thought Margaret, we can all contribute to that subject.

Having four promising topics for her meeting, Margaret searching her memory, knew there were more, but was unable to recall them at this time. Consequently, she set her list aside and began fixing dinner. As her dinner was nearly complete, Santa wandered into the kitchen and asked, "Shall I feed the animals while you work on dinner?"

"Oh Hon," answered Margaret, "I've already done that. Why don't you set the table; that would be a help." Finishing this chore, Margaret served dinner.

Their conversations covered Santa's activity for the day because Margaret's focused on nothing but making sandwiches, punch and picking up along with Dolores, the remains.

Margaret then told Santa, "You know Hon, like you I too am looking forward to getting back into business; with the lack of amusement around here, I am getting to be sort of lackadaisical. I can't even remember all the ideas I had the last time I looked forward to going into business. Growing older is not only hard on the body, but there is no letup for the mind."

Agreeing with her, Santa remarked, "You've got that right."

After tidying the kitchen they went for their regular walk with Mewpurr and Snapper. It was then Margaret reminded Santa how pleasant it was to walk with the animals when time permitted; but his mind was on the trip he wanted to make, knowing it wouldn't be long before the children were out of school for their spring break, and he suggested, "Maybe we could go to Ireland with Fred and Donald when they return to bring the children home."

Continuing, Santa injected, "However, I do believe we are going to have to make a trip even sooner to let Phillip and Leon in on what is happening. Would you like that Hon?"

Before giving her a chance to answer, he went on, "And at our next meeting, we hope to come up with a more appropriate name for the Santa Klaus Anonymous business. Alex has even offered a prize to the one who comes up with the best name; I am at a total loss to come up with a derivative."

Telling Santa, "It's great that you are making a contest of sorts out of this name bit. I think it will help to invigorate the personalities of everyone living here and around us." Then Margaret suggested, "We should really take this opportunity and hold, what . . . a party . . . a celebration . . . a festival . . ., that's it, a festival."

Looking at Margaret, Santa said, "You've got it! A festival! That's exactly what we need; something to bring more life into this village. We don't have to go to Ireland to have fun . . ." and Santa stopped as he thought about why he had to make the trip. Then he told Margaret, "Here are some minor thoughts.

Next week, as I mentioned, we'll have a meeting telling everyone about the contest where they can all compete with their created choices for a name to replace Santa Klaus Anonymous. Rather than announcing these names out loud at the meeting, we will tell everyone to put their name on the entry blank we have provided; after we collect the blanks and check their suggestion, we'll tell them the winning name will be announced at the festival.

"Oh Santa," Margaret exclaimed, "that's a wonderful idea and if we make the trip back to Ireland, we can pick up all kinds of goodies; the type that make a festival what a festival should be.

We can bring Leon, Phillip, Nancy back with us, even Mildred . . . and the children, oh what fun! I'm excited just knowing we are going to do this."

Margaret bubbling with excitement caused a reflection of sparkle in Santa's eyes, which projected his element of love for her.

Telling Margaret "I'm going to let you make up the list of items we have to bring back with us and we can take the cart to make certain there's room for everything we will need." Continuing Santa explained, "I'll call a meeting . . . well correction,

Santa's Second Chance

I've already called the meeting; I'll tell everyone what we are going to do, and I just hope they approve. Wait till I tell Alex, I've actually thought of something on my own."

Overriding Santa's comment Margaret followed up with, "I think Alex will be delighted to know we've thought of something by ourselves, though I do hope he doesn't feel left out."

"Oh I don't think he'll feel left out," added Santa, "because he'll have to prepare the grounds, as well as, putting booths in place and whatever else it takes to hold a festival."

Having finished their walk, as badly as Santa wanted to tell Alex about his new project, he decided it best to wait until morning.

The night was young; Margaret and Santa played a game of WORDFORM and when she won the game, they decided it was time to retire as they'd both had a full day.

Santa could hardly wait to go to sleep so he could wake up the next day, and have his discussion with Alex.

When morning came, Santa dressing quickly, finished the breakfast Margaret prepared and went looking for him.

Seeing Alex walking just ahead, Santa called to him, "Wait Alex, I want to talk with you; can you come to my office with me?"

Asking him, "What's up my friend?" he answered, "Alex, wait till you hear what Margaret and I have come up with!"

"And what might that be?" inquired Alex.

"You know the meeting we are going to have next week?" Continuing Santa explained, "At this meeting, I will tell everyone after we have passed out entry blanks, which . . . by the way, did Vivian say she would accept the new secretarial position? If so, tell her we will need her expertise to draw up entry blanks . . . now back to the meeting.

If everyone, that means all of your comrades, will place the business name they have created on the entry blanks we give them, we will collect and take them with us. While we are in Ireland, we will study the names and decide on a winner. Having made our choice, Margaret and I will shop for and plan the festival that will take place once we return home.

I will have Leon and Phillip make up a large sign, displaying the new business name we have chosen along with the name of the winner, which will be displayed at the festival after the games, etc . . . , etc . . . , etc . . .!

After we return to Ireland, a visit to the post office to register the new name will be in order and they can start putting their advertising together while we decide how we want to handle the details.

At this time, I think Fred and Donald will have to go along with us as we make arrangements enabling them to cope with the design of various projects; and also to show them procedures regarding the collection of mail, as well as making various contacts.

How am I doing so far Alex?" asked Santa and his answer was a repeat of what he previously told him; "Now is the time when you are going to wonder why everyone is so far behind. You are doing just great.

Tell me," asked Alex, "is there anything in particular that I can help with."

"Of course!" and Santa's look of approval included a big smile, as he told him, "You are always such a great help, that sometimes I hesitate to ask you to do any more, but we need some booths set up for the festival.

I thought I'd have Margaret make up a list of what or how many she thinks we'll need. By next week, when we hold our meeting, I'll be able to give you an estimate, if you have no objection."

"Santa," Alex answered, "Your dream is my wish . . . .
For not only the heavens
Will be able to see . . . .
Just how glorious . . . .
This all will be!"

Being puzzled by Alex's answer, but knowing his project was in the hands of one who knew more than he, Santa was certain no matter what, this outcome was . . . .

MEANT TO BE

CONCERNING RESPONSIBILITY

The next day, making notes regarding the Festival, Margaret wrote hurriedly and at random while attaching names to each project.

CAKE WALK - Margaret and Mildred

CLOWNS - Assembly of Elves

DART GAMES - Santa and Dorothy

RACES - Bernard and Elves

FORTUNE TELLER/PALM READER – Gypsy

BARBEQUE - Fred and Donald

GYMNASTICS SHOW – Rex

TALENT SHOW - Jean, Joan and Gerald and Jayne

BAKERY SALE - Margaret and Mildred

ANIMAL PARADE - Patrick, Ralph and Jake

NAMING CONTEST - Santa, Leon and Phillip

Having approximately twelve different events lined up for the festival, Margaret now had to decide in which part of the village they would be held.

The new barn could be used for the Gymnastics Show by leaving the reindeer outside after the animal parade.

Setting up tables and benches from the workshop would allow the barbequing to be cooked at the grounds. The Cake Walk should take place in the street closest to the Bakery Booth and the races should be held on the grounds behind the castle, thus leaving the need for a booth where the Dart Games could be played. Maybe that is where we should hold everything thought

Margaret, in the area behind the castle.

The Talent Show could be held in the open and the Elves Parade could precede the Animal Parade. The Clowns didn't need a booth because they could dress in their quarters, so the only one left needing a booth would be the Fortune Teller/Palm Reader.

Talking to herself Margaret said, "Let me see, I think I'll just rearrange this whole affair. The first activity will be the Elves Parade, followed by the Animal Parade directly to the grounds behind the castle.

We will need a large slab of concrete on which we can set up a stage and Alex can place the booths alongside of it; one for the Bakery Sale, one for the Fortune Teller, and one for the Dart Games."

Continuing, Margaret made an inventory of supplies to be brought from Ireland along with, balloons, ribbons, enough meat for barbequing, baking goods, prizes for the Talent Show, the races, and the Dart Games, with darts and dart boards added to the list.

She continued talking out loud, muttering, "I'll have to get some kind of glass ball for the fortune teller, and maybe a new deck of cards."

Wondering, Margaret questioned in her mind how Santa was going to accept spending all this money. Oh well, it's either here at home or in Ireland she thought, and we can't take it with us. "Besides, it shouldn't be long before we begin to prosper; and isn't that what this is all about?", she uttered.

As Margaret finished her statement, Santa happened to walk in and hearing her words, nonchalantly asked, "What is this all about?"

Not wanting to elude him, Margaret responded, "Hon, do you realize how much this escapade is going to cost us?"

"I know it's, going to be expensive" he answered, "but Margaret let's be realistic. Alex's comrades have given up quite a lot of themselves to stay with us through all these years. Yes, we've fed them, but we haven't paid them and they have not asked for this consideration; they provide their own amusement, and work hard . . . it's time for our friends to play hard, even if it is at our expense.

You know Hon, we can't take it with us and there's no way in which we could have enhanced this beautiful area without their help. I think this is only a partial reward for all they have provided. If we move along with a positive attitude, we may even want to look for more of these elves.

What I'm really anxious to see is the response to 'Santa Klaus Anonymous'. Will it be a success or will it become a fad; like so many other things! Alex thinks this is a great idea for starters, but where do we go after we get it started . . . how do we finish it?"

Feeling Santa's uneasiness regarding the interpretation of his creation, Margaret in an effort to strengthen his understanding said, "Hon, don't ever forget to believe in the strange ways of the Lord. He brought you this far, he's not going to let you fail. He is going to help you finish what you started. His help will be there when you are at the finish line. Otherwise, he might never have sent Alex to assist you."

"I know you're right Margaret, He not only sent Alex, He also sent you! And you have been a real Godsend," responded Santa.

"Flattery," commented Margaret, "will get you everywhere,

but genuinely speaking, don't you know we have a mutual admiration taking place between us?"

"Yes Dear," answered Santa, "but who is cooking today, you or I?"

"I'll cook," said Margaret, "Having worked on this festival most of the day, I need a break."

"Okay, I'll tell you what! Would you like to invite Alex to dinner? We can talk over the festival, clue him in on what we'd like to do and get his opinion?" asked Santa.

"Good idea," remarked Margaret. Tell me, what's his favorite dish?"

Trying to recall Santa told her, "I don't know what you call it, but you know the broiled lamb with the Bernaise Sauce you created? He loves that dish."

"Then that's what we shall have, and it is called 'Lamb Elegante'," responded Margaret.

"I can taste it already," Santa said, running his tongue over his lips and murmuring, "Um . . . um . . ." as he left the room to search for Alex.

Thinking he would find him in the workshop, Alex just happened to be coming out the door as Santa approached him and asked, "Now where are you off to?"

"I was coming to tell you," replied Alex, "regarding Vivian and the job you offered her as secretary to the group of men needing help . . ., she has accepted your offer, and also to ask, where we can set up an office from which she can work."

Hearing this pleasing response Santa suggested, "Why don't we go over to the post office and take a look at the space available; let's see what we can do to find a room for her office."

Walking up the stairs of the post office, Santa reminded Alex, "When we originally partitioned this floor, we made an office for Margaret, but I think we should put Vivian in that office. We have more than enough room in the castle to give Margaret her own space. I never did tell Margaret we'd made a place for her in the post office and then, when I had my attack, everything went wrong. Now that we are returning to normal, I think Margaret deserves her very own office so she doesn't have to spend all of her time in the kitchen." Approvingly, Alex remarked, "You're right Santa; tell me where we can put it, and consider it done."

"By the way Alex," Santa concluded, "I almost forgot! Margaret and I thought you might like to have dinner with us this evening. She's fixing your favorite dish; at the same time, she can let you in on what we are planning for the festival. She really has some great ideas; will you join us?" asked Santa.

"I'd love to, answered Alex, "Shall I come as I am or should I wear my tux?"

"If you want to don your tux," Santa proclaimed, "I'll roll out the red carpet," and they both laughed as they returned to the castle.

By this time, Margaret had the table set and welcomed Alex as if she hadn't seen him in years; she was happy to have his presence, not only for dinner but to be able to explain her plan of action. She asked Santa and Alex to take their seats; the first thing they did was to say prayers.

Pouring a glass of burgundy for each, Santa afforded them an opportunity to toast Alex's health and well being, as well as, their love for one another.

Serving each a plate with an open faced muffin carrying lettuce and slices of tomato, covered by a lamb pattie that had been specially prepared, broiled and sliced in two, Margaret covered it with Bernaise Sauce. Finishing her last bite and swallowing her final drop of wine, she began detailing her plan out loud, but first she told Alex, "I'm so glad you could come to dinner tonight. I not only wanted to share our friendship, but I had an ulterior motive; and I wanted to explain to you what we had in mind for the festival we are promoting.

Your comrades," Margaret went on, "as Santa and I have discussed, have worked so hard and faithfully, we want to do something special for them.

Back when Santa and I went to Ireland with my family for that holiday, which was so exciting, we wondered, even fantasized a bit, about bringing some of that fun to Santa Land for all of your comrades and our friends to enjoy. I've made up a list of activities and we want everyone to join in, not only Fred's and Donald's family, but all of your comrades, the animals and anyone who helped to make Santa Land the great village it is."

Looking at Santa Margaret asked Alex, "Am I rambling too much?"

Being the gentleman he was Alex said, "No Margaret, I'm anxious to hear your plan. It sounds like . . . not only something different, but like the fun we've been missing all these years because we have been so involved in work."

Expecting Margaret to elaborate on the description of what they had in mind Santa told Margaret, "You're doing fine Dear, just continue with our plans." Retrieving her list Margaret explained everything in as much detail as possible.

Being a perceptive person, Alex didn't miss a word. When she finished, he was not only amazed, but realized why Santa wanted Margaret to have her own office. Alex was able to see what an articulate person she was. Everything appeared clear as to what they needed, and what he had to do, to comply with Margaret's and Santa's position . . . .

CONCERNING RESPONSIBILITY

ALWAYS BELIEVE

With the next meeting being days away Santa tried to subdue his anxiety knowing his pet project was so involved.

Margaret was wondering if a meeting with Mary and Dorothy should wait until after the festivities. Thinking ahead, she knew she would need as much cooperation as she could gather from them, feeling they were an important aspect to the success of the festival. For this reason, Margaret invited Dorothy and Mary to attend a meeting in the Conference Room which was still three days prior to Santa holding his next get-together.

While thinking of this affair, Margaret decided her thoughts required action. Changing her mind about a meeting in the Conference Room, she found herself at the girl's front door.

Answering the door, Mary led Margaret through the vestibule to the family room while asking, "And to what do we owe the honor of this visit?"

Ignoring what sounded like a stock question whenever someone answered the front door, Margaret replied, "Mary, I wondered if you or Dorothy have heard anything about the festival Santa and I are about to arrange? I know he didn't mention it at his last assembly, but when he holds his next meeting, he's going to announce the details to everyone.

You see, he is going to hold a 'Naming Contest', which will involve all of our friends and comrades in the village. You are the first to know, and I want you to feel free to be creative in entering your ideas. After you have filled out an entry blank and turned it in along with all of the others, we will study the names and announce the winner at the festival.

This festival will involve all sorts of activities, from cake-walks to races, parades, games even fortune telling. Do I have your attention yet?" asked Margaret.

Always anxious to be heard, Dorothy inquired, "And where are you going to hold this festival?"

Answering Margaret told her, "On the grounds behind the castle where Alex will set up booths and a stage while we are gone . . ."

Not getting a chance to complete her sentence, Mary interrupted with, "Gone . . . where are you off to?"

Knowing the comment she made was a mistake, Margaret listened as Dorothy followed up with, "Are we all going on this trip?"

Trying to avoid a direct invitation to Mary and Dorothy, whom she felt wanted to accompany she and Santa, Margaret told them, "To tell you the truth I'm not certain what Santa has in mind. I only know, we have a lot of items to bring back from Ireland for the festival. We also thought we might bring back the children, who will be out of school by that time for spring vacation, along with Leon, Phillip, Nancy and Mildred. Santa did not anticipate taking the cart, and if Fred and Donald come along, as I'm sure he expects them to for business purposes, there will barely be enough room for all of us, the necessities we have to pickup for home and the festival, as well as fitting everyone into the sleigh. There will be no time for fun, games or entertainment. Besides, that will all happen when we return home; and we don't want to be so tired we can't enjoy the festival."

There, Margaret had said it all; her description came out short, sweet, and to the point. What more could she add?

Mary concluded, "We get it; you want the men all to yourself."

"Yes," Margaret remarked sarcastically, "the men . . . the children, the chores and all the detail."

To help Margaret feel at ease, Dorothy commented, "That's okay Margaret; any time you want to pawn them off on me, I'll be glad to have them, especially Santa."

Responding, Margaret told her, "Dorothy, I wouldn't give up Santa for anything; I'm very happy to be able to call him my own.

Back to our meeting," Margaret went on, "Are you guys in or out? We have only a few days left to do this, or maybe we should wait until our return from Ireland. In that way, we'll have a better idea of exactly what's going on and who's needed where. What I really need to confirm is, can I count on you two?" she asked.

Both Dorothy and Mary agreed, "Of course, you can!" With this response Margaret concluded, "I needed your assurance, and since that's settled, I'd better be on my way."

Bidding Margaret farewell, Dorothy added, "Take care of the children and we'll see you when you return, if not sooner!"

Margaret was happy to know they were all in agreement. Thinking she might have to conduct the festival alone, she was certain there would be plenty of assistance from Santa's helpers. However, they were there for pleasure not work; besides, she needed a different kind of help.

Returning to the kitchen to make a list of all the odds and ends they would have to bring home, she also had to remember to ask Dolores to take care of Mewpurr and Snapper.

Margaret was not taking any chance of bringing them along and possibly finding Mewpurr behaving in a repeat performance like that of the previous vacation trip she enjoyed so well.

Margaret's spare time allowed her to begin packing bags. Knowing they were not going to stay long, she was aware they would still need changes of clothing.

Hours grew into days and time gave way to Santa's meeting. The whole village looked forward to hearing about the details of the Naming Contest, as well as the festival to be held upon the committees return from Ireland.

As the meeting began Santa explained to the villagers, "Right now, we have a committee who will be reviewing this whole affair. Should there be any questions, you can ask anyone of them for an answer. This committee will consist of Alfonso, Alfred, Donald, Fred, Leon, Phillip, Nancy and of course, you all know my wife Margaret, as well as, yours truly. To make the contest more challenging, we will not allow any of the committee members, or their families, to participate in the Naming Contest. Since we are all going to be judges, we feel it is inappropriate to compete with your entries.

May I remind you, should there be a need for more than one blank, just ask for extras! We will award a prize for a first place name, as well as, second place and a runner-up; the rest is up to you. These entry blanks will be collected and we will take them with us to review and decide the best choice of a name to replace 'Santa Klaus Anonymous'."

The room filled with excitement as everyone completed their entry blanks with what they hoped would be the winning name.

Having collected the forms, Santa put them in a bag and sealed it tightly, lest any should be lost.

Santa's Second Chance

Continuing on about the festival he said, "First, there will be a variety of activities." With a list given to him by Margaret, he tried to explain how the festival would be conducted.

"We will have a parade of elves, some dressed as clowns and some in costumes. It is up to you to decide which you want to be, or how you would like to dress. Behind your comrades will be the Animal Parade; the festival will be held on the grounds in back of the castle. There will be three booths close to the sides of the stage Alex is going to build while we are gone. One booth will be for a Bakery Sale, one for a Fortune Teller/Palm Reader, and the third booth will have a Dart Game. So, sharpen your skills to be all you can be."

Continuing, Santa explained, "The children will be on vacation, and they will perform in a Gymnastics Show, directed by Rex. We will also have a Talent Show, and Cake Walks, in which you can win baked goods. There will be races, and it will be up to you to pick your own team. Fred and Donald will be barbequing and last but not least, we will be announcing the winner of the Naming Contest. You will have three more days in which to finish your entry blanks.

Once again, I've honed in on most everything and we will probably be gone for near to a week so you will have enough time to prepare for these events; let's make the most of it, and I wish you all GOOD LUCK!"

As the elves filed out of the Conference Room, Fred decided to voice his disappointment to Santa about not being allowed to participate in the Naming Contest.

Santa explained to Fred, how hard they (the elves) had worked and how important it was to give their morale a boost now and then; this was the time to help improve as well as set the atmosphere for the festival to come.

"Remember," Santa said, "these people are your helpers; do you want me to pay them out of your bonuses, when you get them?"

Fred cocked his head, and upon hearing Santa announce. "Pay out of your bonus," he knew Santa was right; but trying to throw a shadow of doubt over the whole operation regarding bonuses Fred inquired, "Santa are you sure there will be bonuses?"

Santa's response to Fred's question just before he left the Conference Room was, "If you want to make it happen, work hard, and . . . believe."

Dorothy and Mary were upset when they heard that, because they were family members of the committee, they would not be allowed to enter the Naming Contest. They even confronted Margaret, reminding her of what she had proclaimed when they first discussed the festival; but being steadfast in defending Santa's rules, she replied, "I m sorry, but Santa and I did not discuss the regulations of the program. I was out of line when I gave you incorrect information not knowing the details. Unfortunately, there is nothing we can do about this situation; besides are we not all adults here?" questioned Margaret.

Unhappy with the final outcome, Margaret, as far as she was concerned would not have the last word. Being devious as she sometimes could be Dorothy said to Mary after Margaret's departure, "You know, I have noticed something unusual. I'll bet if I exposed the parties and projects involved, right under our noses, I could get Santa to change his mind about that ruling, rather than to have this matter made public."

Questioning Dorothy, Mary suspiciously asked, "You don't

mean 'Blackmail'?"

Responding to Mary's question, she said, "Well, not exactly!" Continuing Dorothy explained, "Mary, have you ever noticed, whenever Santa wants anything built, he commissions Alex to do the building and then goes away on a trip someplace; when he returns, it's complete . . . finished . . . done! Has it ever occurred to you . . . or let me put it this way," she went on, "where do you suppose all of those materials come from? You never see Santa bringing them from Ireland. And no one else visits or brings the kind of materials it takes to build, barns . . . post offices . . . weather towers . . . maybe even this castle . . .""

By this time, Mary had heard enough and she told Dorothy, "Say no more."

Persisting Dorothy questioned, "Don't you want to get your choice of names into the 'Naming Contest'?"

Replying, Mary stated, "Dorothy, I will not have any part of your chicanery. Besides, what makes you think you have a winning name? Don't forget, there is a lot of competition out there; and you know what else? These elves are ingenious. They may look small, but they are mighty.

Another thing," Mary continued, "What kind of prize do you suppose Santa is going to present? It isn't going to be money . . . so . . . I think it's best you just forget the whole matter."

Dorothy, not wanting to cause trouble outwardly, pretended to let it go; but knowing in her own mind, she was going to form a plan to prove she was right, even if only to Mary.

When Fred and Donald returned from Santa's meeting they told their wives they needed bags packed, to be ready and waiting for the next trip to Ireland. Their report turned the trip into strictly business. They also mentioned bringing the children home, since school would soon let out for spring vacation.

Before going to sleep that night, Dorothy approached Fred, and told him about her plan of action.

Responding Fred asked Dorothy without reservation, "Why would you want to do something like that?

Santa has told us there would be bonuses; and since I returned all of Margaret's household goods, I am back in her good graces; you don't want to spoil our new found relationship." The last thing Fred said before he let out his first snooze was, "Dorothy, I absolutely forbid it!"

But Dorothy, being the Dorothy she was, said to herself, "Looks like I'll have to go it alone!"

Her persistence was as strong as her determination, and she just couldn't let go. The plan she formed was to let everyone think she had discarded the whole idea. Actually, she was just waiting for a spur of the moment chance to spring forward, and hopefully, trap someone in a sly act.

Going to sleep, Dorothy looked forward to a dream world that would help her form a plan to her liking because she could not . . .

ALWAYS BELIEVE

A SUCCESS IN THE MAKING

Earlier in the evening, at the Klaus residence, Margaret relayed the events of the day to Santa and he found them very interesting.

Then he said to Margaret, "Suppose we take the cart and bring Mary and Dorothy along with us. They will be able to see what's going on and they can help you shop, while I take charge of Fred and Donald to acquaint them with postal regulations. We can use them to help us read the names for the contest, and since they are family members of the committee, they can help with the judging."

Thinking Santa had the answer to the problem, the next day, Margaret decided to tell the ladies of his proposal. Expecting them to be overjoyed because she knew, they didn't want to stay home while everyone was in Ireland, having a good time (they thought), she couldn't wait till the next day, so she ran upstairs to tell Mary and Dorothy the good news.

Knowing Dorothy would be unhappy about this surprise because she felt it might spoil whatever happened to be her latest plan of action, Mary nevertheless told Margaret, "I know she'll just love to come along; I'll talk her into it, and everything will be just fine. I do know that I for one will be looking forward to this trip, so count me in and when do we leave?"

"About the parting date," Margaret maintained, "I'm not certain, but I know it's going to be soon. I'll get back to you after I double check with Santa."

Looking for Santa, Margaret found him searching for her.

He told her, "I'm going to do one more collection of names or I should say, Alex is going to do the collection and then we will be on our way if not tomorrow, the day after. I really want to get the advertising into progress so we can get started on our project.

I've decided the prize for the 'Naming Contest' should be a trophy; as a matter of fact, three trophies; one for the winner, one for second place and one for the runner up. In this way, there will be no jealousy regarding who got a bigger and better prize.

Once Alex brings me the rest of the entry blanks, we'll be ready for our trip; I'll tell Fred and Donald so they can give the news to Mary and Dorothy to be ready and waiting."

The next morning, with the fog zooming in on their take-off point, Santa decided that even with the fog his reindeer being familiar enough with the route, wouldn't have any problems making the trip.

In spite of her mischievous attitude, Dorothy and Mary, along with Fred and Donald arrived at the take-off port, and saw the sleigh hooked up to the cart, carrying the committee members.

Santa along with Margaret waiting in the sleigh, told Alex after he placed the bag of entry blanks in the cart, the cement he would need for the slab of concrete to produce the stage could be found in the old barn.

Making certain everyone heard him and knowing the business at hand would be taken care of Santa called to his reindeer, "Let's GO GUYS," and they were on their way!

The trips between Santa Land and Ireland seemed to be getting shorter; possibly because the reindeer were traveling at a faster rate of speed. Consequently the group found themselves at their destination, once again in the dark of the early morning.

Santa's Second Chance

Santa led the reindeer into the barn, and everyone filed out of the sleigh into the house, where they found Leon, Phillip, Nancy and Mildred, along with the children sleeping soundly.

Of course no one knew that Santa, Fred and Donald, along with the rest of the party, were returning to Ireland to take up renewal of the business project, for which they had originally been sent.

Margaret was not surprised to find the house so neatly taken care of and the time for the children to wake and prepare for school was near. To give Mildred a break from her routine duties, Margaret announced that she would begin preparing breakfast.

The noise from the travelers in the kitchen brought Mildred out of her room along with Nancy. They were both thrilled to see Santa and Margaret. The looks on their faces gave way to the emotion they felt upon seeing their comrades with Alfonso and Alfred among them. There was a lot of welcoming, hugging, kissing, and before it was over, the children, had awakened to find their parents, whom they really were not expecting to see.

As Mildred and Nancy set the table, two other sleepyheads entered the room, namely Leon and Phillip. They were a little bewildered, but nevertheless, thrilled to learn of Santa's recovery and to know they were going to be more than caretakers. The work on the project they were originally sent to promote, was once again going to commence.

During breakfast, Santa made it clear that this evening after dinner, they would hold a meeting to organize the tasks regarding the festival confronting them, as well as, seeking a name for 'Santa Klaus Anonymous' with an easier, more business-like sound.

"At this time," Santa proclaimed, "we will set down rules and regulations regarding how and what we want to achieve and decide the answers to a whole lot of questions that will come into play, as well as advertising for this idea. After the meeting this evening, we will all have to buckle down and work hard to make this trip worth the problems we are going to encounter.

This afternoon, Margaret and I have some shopping to do; you Fred and Donald, along with your wives, feel free to use your time as you please."

Feeling very competent, Fred asked Santa when they would be going to register at the post office?

Knowing this was an important part of their trip, Santa answered, "Maybe if you fellows are going to be anywhere in the vicinity of the post office, you could pick up some applications for us and we can complete them together at the meeting. In this manner, we will all know what is happening, and we can devise a plan so the right hand will know exactly what the left hand is doing. I dare say with this accomplished, we should be able to go about business very quickly without having to ask one another for answers; we should be able to work together very smoothly."

Santa and Margaret went grocery shopping while everyone else went in their chosen directions.

As they shopped in the Produce Department, Margaret had a bright idea, and then suggested it telling Santa, "I've just had a great notion for prizes. Look at those beautiful fruit baskets, the ones packed in cellophane and tied with the pretty ribbons and bows. Wouldn't they make wonderful prizes? We could use one of the larger baskets for second place in the 'Naming Contest' and the smaller basket for the runner-up. We don't have to buy them today we'll just come back and order them so they will be ready on the day before we are going to leave for home."

Santa agreed that this was a great idea, leaving them with only knick-knacks to be concerned about; but then when Margaret also came up with sausages, big and little for prizes at the dart booth and races, the Best Costume Competition, the Talent Contest . . ., Santa broke in with, "Maybe some of the prizes but not all of them."

Answering him Margaret commented, "How about asking the others what they think, and like the fruit baskets, we can pick them up later."

"Good enough," agreed Santa.

Having finished their grocery shopping, they went to a novelty store where they would be able to locate their other needs.

Spying the glass balls she needed for the fortune teller, while looking at an assortment of gadgets, Margaret put two of them into her cart. She and Santa proceeded down aisle after aisle, picking up a novelty here and there till they decided they'd had enough. The contents of their cart would fill three shopping bags.

Commenting, Santa told Margaret, "I think this is enough. We have a whole storeroom full of items we could give away as gifts and wouldn't even have to purchase or bring them back from Ireland."

Being on the practical side Margaret said, "I think you're right Hon; so let's just take the items we don't make in Santa Land and if we need anymore prizes, we can find them at home." Paying for their purchases, they quickly returned to the house.

By this time, Mildred and Nancy had taken it upon themselves to prepare dinner. With everyone present, all looked forward to the meeting afterwards.

Having a flashback to the last time they tried to hold this meeting, Santa remembered how disastrous it became, but this time, he felt very encouraged about a . . . . .

A SUCCESS IN THE MAKING

MATTERS OF THE FESTIVAL

The meeting called for after dinner had finally come. Everyone gathered at the dining room table which was eventually called the Conference Table.

Asking Nancy to bring along a pad of paper and pencils so they could take notes, with hers being regarded as the Minutes of the Meeting, Santa brought the bag of entries which had been submitted by Alex's comrades for the contest.

Holding the greatest suspense for all was the new name to be chosen entered into the 'Naming Contest' to replace the 'Santa Klaus Anonymous' name.

Calling the meeting to order, Santa explained to everyone, "We have many subjects to cover this evening, and we may not even be able to touch on everything; but most important on the list is the 'Naming Contest' because without a business name for our group, we have no business."

There he went again, getting all twisted in his words, but this time he didn't have Alex to help, so he said to himself, "Okay Santa, just deal with it," and this he did.

Opening the bag full of names, he told everyone, "I will pass these names out to each of you until there are no more to be had."

Looking as if everyone had at least five names setting in front of them, Santa then said, "I want each of you to read a name out loud. We will listen, take it into consideration and go on to the next name. When you hear a name that you think sounds appropriate, write it on your piece of paper, and when we finish with all of the entries, we will review what you felt were the best choices."

Beginning the process Margaret called out, " 'Santas Bloomers' " and then came, 'Santa's Angels' followed by 'Santa's Projection Group'. 'Santa's Flying Squadron', was the next announcement, with 'Growing Santas' to follow; then, 'Super Santas' . . . 'Adopt-A- Santa' . . . at this point Santa remarked to himself, "I think they have the wrong idea . . .," but he continued to listen as Alfonso announced, " 'Santas With A Purpose'. . ." next, 'Mobile Santas' and then came, 'Santas Replacement Corp'.

'Santas Reserve Group' made it evident to Santa, that besides being able to get a laugh out of some of these creations, the entrants did not realize what he was looking for, but as requested everyone kept on presenting their names, and the next was 'The Flying Santas'.

That sounds a little better thought Santa, since that's what they could be.

Ridiculous names kept popping up like, 'Santas In Red' . . . 'Santas On Call' . . . 'Traveling Santas' . . . 'Santas Renaissance' . . . 'Santas Helpers' . . . (He already had helpers that could never be Santa he thought, but an opinion he was careful not to express.) 'Blossoming Santas' . . . 'Be All You Can Santas' . . . 'Santas Flying Squadron'. . . 'Santas Brigade' . . . (too militaristic he thought) 'Santa's Air Reserve'.

Then came a name, 'Santas Airways Group' . . . that appealed to Santa, and sounded business like, as well as most fitting for the purpose, but he wasn't the deciding factor.

Santa's Second Chance

Wanting the participation of everyone at this meeting, Santa asked them to voice their opinions by first, raising their hands and then, calling out their choices. Five of the group raised their hands and Santa chose Fred to be the first to speak.

Never known to be shy, Fred spoke up saying, "I think everyone has done a tremendous job, and there are several names I feel are outstanding."

Santa, immediately asked, "And what might they be?"

Fred, knowing he was going to be a big part of the operation remarked, "Well I like the 'Flying Santas'."

Commenting, "That's good Fred," since it was also one of his favorites,

Santa went on asking, "How about you, Leon?" and he answered, "Business wise, I think 'Santas Airways Group' would make a big hit!"

"All right Leon, and what about you Phillip, what do you think," continued Santa. He replied, I prefer 'Santa's Air Reserve', but maybe as a division, not for the name of a business; it again sounds too military-ish."

Nancy preferred, 'The Flying Santas'.

Next Santa asked, "And your preference Donald?" Standing up, Donald agreeing with Leon said, "I like the 'Santas Airways Group'," and sat down.

"Okay," responded Santa, "I'll tell you what we'll do. We seem to think alike and I have my thoughts about which I feel are best, so I will call out three of the names you mentioned, and we will take a vote.

The first name is, 'The Flying Santas'," and the show of

hands told Santa there were five votes. Again he said, "How about, 'Santa's Air Reserve?' and only three hands went up for that choice.

"Sounding like a really proper name is, 'Santas Airways Group'," declared Santa and with this announcement all hands went up. It appeared to be a unanimous decision, and the name they all agreed upon to replace 'Santa Klaus Anonymous' would be, 'Santas Airways Group'.

Santa continued to report, "In second place, we have, 'The Flying Santas', with 'Santa's Air Reserve' becoming our runner-up. Now that we have a name we will be able to finish the application forms for the mail delivery and get on to other business."

Passing the applications Fred had picked up at the post office on to Nancy, Santa asked her to complete them with the necessary information and give them back to Fred so he could return them to the proper authorities.

It had been a long active day for most, and Santa suggested they continue this meeting in the morning with fresh, clear minds so they would be able to evaluate the name they had chosen.

Calling the meeting for 10:00 A.M., Santa saw everyone up quite early. Having finished breakfast with time to spare, they began to gather around the Conference Table.

There was a buzz among them, but as Santa entered the room he noticed it grew unusually quiet. While this did not bother him, he could feel an omen of something waiting to happen, like the dark before the dawn. Neither he nor Margaret suspected anything unusual so Santa said, "If you are all wide awake with bushy tails," everyone thought he was trying to be funny, "we will begin our meeting."

Santa's Second Chance

Blushing because he did not mean to infer they had bushy tails, everyone laughed and he continued, "I want to welcome you all to the new 'Santas Airways Group'; and I might ask if anyone has any questions?"

Raising his hand Leon asked, "Santa, we've managed to decide on new names with first, second and third place winners, but you collected the entry blanks so quickly, we never thought to ask who had submitted them?"

Answering him, Santa replied, "Leon, yesterday was such a long day, I never thought of looking at the entrant's name on the blanks and for now, I've left the bag with all the entries in my room. Having been so happy to have decided on a name, I wasn't thinking, but when we take a break for lunch, I'll retrieve the bag and we'll find out who it was."

Unknown to Santa, there was one sitting at the table who knew the name of the winner, but that one was not about to disclose the identity. That one would wait for Santa to bring the information to the group.

Santa's next subject involved distributing the prizes for the first, second and third place winners.

"As you know, the first place winner will receive a trophy; the second and third place winner will receive fruit baskets. Margaret and I will order them tomorrow so they will be available to pick up and take back with us when we are ready to return to Santa Land."

"Nancy," Santa proclaimed, " if you will let us know when you have completed the paperwork for the post office, I will go with Fred and Donald to register the necessary information."

Continuing, Santa disclosed, "Margaret and I have discussed having the mail delivered here to the house, which will make it easier for Fred and Donald to pick up.

Now, for the advertising Leon and Phillip will prepare before we leave, I need your suggestions as to the interviewing of applicants applying for Santa positions."

Raising his hand Fred suggested, "I propose we set a date, and you do the interviewing Santa because it is you they will have to resemble. Well, I don't mean resemble, I should say it is you they will have to learn to represent."

"I agree," answered Santa, "but I need someone to volunteer to make out the applications they must fill out before being interviewed."

At this time, Margaret spoke up saying, "I can do that Santa . . . who knows you better than I? I'll cover all of the requisites." Accepting her offer, he responded, "The job is yours!

Next question on the agenda," Santa inquired, "where do we hold the school at which they can be trained?"

Rising with an answer to this question, Donald proposed, "It would be appropriate to bring them back to Santa Land so they could have the experience of flying by themselves. After all they will be flying by themselves one day, will they not?" he questioned.

Not being certain he wanted them to be involved with the aspects of reindeer Santa told Donald, "At this time, it's a bit premature for them to be concerned with flying encounters. Yes, I do think we should bring them to Santa Land for schooling because there will be so many other facets of the operation with which they must become familiar; I want them to know the business from inside and out. Besides, it will be easier to have them in Santa Land, where there is room for all, rather than trying to school them in the house."

Santa's Second Chance

Having a question to ask, Mary raised her hand inquiring, "Santa, do you have any idea what these men will wear?"

Knowing exactly what he could tell her, first he asked, "Mary, do you remember when Margaret and I married and Margaret had sewn that beautiful red suit for me to wear on our wedding day? Well, I think, for some unknown reason, that suit was very significant, as well as, a sign of great things to come.

I think Santas Airways Group will be one of the greatest creations for mankind, now . . . and lasting for a long time. . . possibly for decades. How Margaret knew this would someday mean something, I'll never know . . ."

As Margaret listened, she interrupted with, "I didn't know . . . , this was just another one of those, 'strange ways of the Lord' or maybe just a coincidence."

Then Mary asked, "Well, who will sew the suits for the men?"

Santa's confirmation told her, "I'm certain we can find someone back in Santa Land who knows a bit about tailoring; but Mary, how about if you take on this job and work with the one, I'm sure Alex will recommend to help with this project?"

"I'm willing as long as you can furnish the help," answered Mary. "Are you getting all of this down on paper Nancy?" questioned Santa; and as she nodded her head, Santa noticed that Mildred left the group to fix lunch. Realizing how the time had flown, Santa agreed to adjourn the meeting till after lunch at 1:00 P.M.

Instead of waiting with the group for lunch, Santa went back to his room to get the bag of entry forms so he could look for the one that carried the winning name, as well as, the two that became second and third place winners.

Sitting at his desk, Santa spilled out the contents of the bag, covering his desk top with entry blanks. Quickly sifting through them he scanned each one, looking for the necessary three. "Ah!" he said, "Here are the numbers two and three winners," but the first place winner was nowhere to be found.

Puzzled, because he knew he had gathered all of the entry blanks available, Santa again checked the papers in front of him, but could not find one carrying the name they had chosen, 'Santas Airways Group'.

Now what he thought, as his mind reverted to the night before, when he first heard the name and who it was that read it aloud. If he remembered correctly, it was Alfonso. Thinking ahead, he said to himself, "I suppose I'll have to ask him what happened to the entry blank as it definitely doesn't seem to be here."

Santa set the other two entry blanks aside, put the rest of the names back into the bag and joined the rest of the group for the tasty lunch Mildred had prepared and about which everyone raved.

Noticing it was time to get back to their meeting, Santa decided first to have a private session with Alfonso. He asked Alfonso to join him in his room where they could sit down and talk freely, before they returned to continue the meeting.

Following Santa into his room Alfonso watched him pick up the bag filled with entry blanks and again emptied its contents onto the desk top.

Looking at Alfonso, he said, "I am totally baffled by what has happened here, and the reason I needed to have this discussion with you is . . ., Alfonso, you were the one who read the entry blank carrying the first place name; but of all these entries, only that one seems to be missing. Do you remember what you did with it after you read the name?"

Sitting speechless, Alfonso scratched his head and then responded, "You know Santa, I was sitting next to Dorothy, and after I read the name, I set it down and never thought about the person who wrote it since this was not in question at the time; I do recall seeing Dorothy pick it up and the rest is a blank. Whether she returned it or not, I cannot say."

Santa wanting to get on with the meeting said, "I would rather you didn't mention this problem, and I suppose I will have to ask Dorothy about the matter. For now, we had better get back to the meeting.

I will also hold off mentioning the names of the winners until after dinner. Maybe by that time, I'll know who it was." They returned to the conference table where everyone was waiting to carry on with . . .

MATTERS OF THE FESTIVAL

Irene Zulueta

FROM ANONYMOUS

TO ANONYMOUS

Before calling the meeting to order Santa announced, "Because of circumstances beyond my control at this time, we will wait until we return to Santa Land to give you the names of the winning entrants in the Naming Contest.

In this way it will be a real surprise for everyone; and I assure you, it will be a topic for conversation! Our festival will be the talk of Santa Land . . ., I hope," he added. "Now, back to the other subjects we have to deal with.

First, we will need people to service booths; we will have a Bakery Booth, Dart Games and the Fortune Teller/Palm Reader Booth. At the same time, we will need a balloon blower, someone to handle the Cake Walk, and let's not forget the Barbeque."

Quickly raising his hand Donald stood up and said, "Fred and I will volunteer for the barbeque."

"That will be fine," replied Santa. "How about the Bakery Booth and Cake Walk?" he asked.

"I think that given Mildred's experience, along with my help, we should have no problem taking care of the Bakery Booth; is that okay with you Mildred?" asked Margaret. "Of course," Mildred agreed, "I'm glad you asked, as you all know, sweets are my forte'."

Nancy was busy making notes, knowing that everyone was anxious to take part in helping Santa provide a meaningful festival.

Santa's Second Chance

Fred raised his hand and said, "I'm sure Patrick will help Jake and Ralph with the Animal Parade," and Nancy added these three prospects to her list.

"Leon and Phillip will be in charge of the Naming Contest since they are developing the ads for the 'Help Wanted' advertisements," announced Santa. Rex of course, will be in charge of the Gymnastics Division for the Talent Show; I suggest we use the children, Jayne, Gerald, Jean and Joan, along with Bernard as judges. At least with their judging, we know, being children they'll give us honest opinions.

For the Dart Games, I will offer my services and take on as a partner . . . how about you, Dorothy?" said Santa. Feeling as if she had no alternative, Dorothy agreed to be his associate.

Asking Nancy if he'd covered everything, her response was, "Who will be in charge of the clowns and balloons?"

"I don't think the clowns will need any help; they can pretty much take care of themselves. However, I suggest Alfonso and Alfred become the balloon blowers," declared Santa. Proposing, because he worked so hard, they make Alex their Grand Marshal for the parade, everyone thought this was a noble gesture and agreed with him. "Won't he be surprised," remarked Phillip.

Deciding the next topic to be addressed should be the Bakery Booth, Santa talked directly to Mildred saying, "I want you to be in charge, but I don't expect you to do all the baking. I would like to have you encourage some of your comrades to bake cakes or cookies, and you also, Dorothy and Mary, as I know Margaret will be only too happy to oblige us.?

I believe we have chosen Gypsy to be our Fortune Teller, though she doesn't know it yet Nancy" added Santa, "and if you will help her when she responds to needing some assistance it would be appreciated."

Santa had a way of asking for favors that made it hard for anyone to say no. It was growing late, so he decided it was time to wrap up their meeting for the day and asked if there were any more subjects to be covered? "If not, I'll see you at dinner.

One other thing," added Santa, "Tomorrow Fred, Donald and I will go to the post office. If there is something special you want to do before we return home, feel free to do it."

When Santa said, "Feel free," Leon and Phillip asked if they could come along; they needed cardstock for the signs they were going to make. Remembering he also needed forms he could complete for the 'Help Wanted' ads printed in the newspapers, Phillip added this to his list.

Dorothy and Mary wanted to go shopping, but they admitted it would only be window shopping because there was no money with which to shop.

Before everyone departed from the room, Santa told Dorothy he would like to have a word with her. Thinking he wanted to discuss the Dart Games booth, she told Mary she'd catch up with her in a little bit.

Then Santa said, "Dorothy, let's go where we can talk privately." Leading her into his room and asking her to take a seat at the desk, he sat across from her.

His first question to Dorothy was, "Do you like it here in Ireland?"

She looked at Santa and answered, "It's positively delightful! I'm so glad you invited us to come along."

"Well, that's good! I'm glad that you're glad," replied Santa, intentionally repeating his words, hoping to put her at ease.

"Now, the reason I need to have this discussion with you . . . yesterday, when we read all the names out loud, it was Alfonso who read the name we decided to use as the first place winner, but no one on the committee asked who had entered the name. Today when I went through the bag, trying to find a blank with the winning name, it came up missing. Consequently, I had to ask Alfonso about it and obviously, in his excitement, he hadn't looked at the name of the winner, because the question never arose. The one thing he did remember was sitting next to you and seeing you pick it up . . ., and then he drew a blank. Tell me Dorothy, is it possible that after you picked it up and didn't put it back down, when I collected the names, it wasn't there to collect?"

Beginning to fidget in her chair. . . Dorothy letting out an "Oh-oh," under her breadth, thought what do I say next? Putting her hand into her pocket as if to empty it, she found a piece of crumpled paper, and almost at once, said to Santa, "My heavens, look at this. Being excited when you announced the name I held in my hand, I must have crumpled it thinking it was a handkerchief, and put it in my pocket. I'm so sorry!" As she handed the piece of paper to Santa, he tried to flatten it so he could read it. Looking at it closely he realized the name of the entrant had been erased.

"Dorothy," Santa said, "you know that family members or anyone serving on the committee was not eligible for the contest, don't you?"

"Well . . . yes," she said sheepishly adding, "and Fred emphatically asked me not to do anything that would jeopardize his relationship with you."

"Well, you did a good job Dorothy, you created a most appropriate name, but I cannot give you the credit you would have received if you were one of Alex's comrades. However, I have no one else to give the credit to, and since the entrant's name has been erased . . ."

At the sound of his statement, Dorothy's whole being fluttered, as she thought Santa was going to have a change of heart and give her the trophy carrying the Gilpatrick name.

Then he said, "The trophy will have to bear the words, 'DONOR ANONYMOUS'.

Now, I can either tell Fred of your shenanigans, or we can make this our secret; it's your choice."

"Santa," Dorothy murmured softly, "I'd rather you didn't mention this to Fred, he's trying so hard to be congenial."

"As you wish," Santa replied, "I've already forgotten our conversation. We've just gone . . .

FROM ANONYMOUS TO ANONYMOUS"

BIRDS OF A FEATHER

The following morning, after finishing breakfast, Santa sat at his desk making a list of all the necessary trips to be made that day. He wondered if Margaret wanted to come along, but he surmised, she probably had an agenda of her own.

The children were at school so he decided to ask Fred and Donald if they would like to set a time for their trip to the post office.

Finding Fred and Donald in the barn enjoying the task of grooming, especially Santa's reindeer, they had hoped someday their own team would be a shining example of what one could do when they put their minds, as well as, a little effort to work on the matter.

Asking Fred and Donald when they would be ready to make the trip to the post office, they told Santa an afternoon jaunt would be ideal so they could have one of Mildred's great lunches before leaving home. Santa confirmed the time and left to look for Margaret.

He found her in the kitchen with Mildred, examining some of her favorite recipes. The two of them had become good friends in a short time. Having written her very own cookbook, Margaret was telling Mildred, perhaps she could have it published, another business idea with which She was toying.

Upon entering the kitchen, Santa asked, "Am I interrupting anything?"

"Not really" replied Margaret. "We were about to make a grocery list for baking supplies to be taken home for the festival."

"Can I assume you don't care to make the trip to the post office with Fred, Donald and myself?" asked Santa.

Knowing they didn't really need her help, Margaret advised him she and Mildred would shop for the necessary groceries.

Remembering the trophy they had to order, Margaret asked Santa about it.

Because he had not shared the dilemma of Dorothy's venture with anyone, he told her, "We should find out when the children will be out of school, and make certain we order it so it will be ready by the time we plan on leaving."

That sounds great," responded Margaret.

Remembering that Leon and Phillip asked about going along on the trip to the post office, Santa returned to the barn to inquire if they still wanted to come along with Fred, he and Donald. Their negative response let Santa off the hook for explaining who or what they were.

All we need," Phillip told Santa, "is some cardstock large enough to make a sign for the Naming Contest, with enough space for three winners; also, if you will, stop by the newspaper office and get the applications needed for placing 'Help Wanted' Ads."

Lunchtime found appetites filled, and the three men started out to the post office, which was right around the corner from where they were staying.

After standing in line for approximately forty-five minutes they finally made it to the counter and found themselves talking to a postal representative.

Explaining why they were there, the postal agent asked for their paperwork. Santa said, "Give the man the paperwork Fred!"

Looking dumbfounded Fred said to Santa, "I don't have the application," and looking at Donald asked, "Do you have the papers?" Waving his hands to show they were empty, Donald said to Santa, "I thought you had them."

By this time the agent had pulled out a new set of papers for them to complete saying, "If you will step aside while you are finishing these papers, I'll help the next customer."

Feeling very foolish for not having checked with them before leaving the house, Santa said, "We might as well go back and get the completed papers; I know Nancy has them. It's a good thing we are staying right around the corner from here."

Out of the post office went three men looking like 'Sad Sacks,' and Santa was totally disgruntled at the lack of attention causing this problem.

As they reached the house, they saw Nancy coming out the front door carrying an envelope in her hands. Seeing the three men, she asked, "Are you looking for this?"

Sounding perturbed, Donald said, "Nancy, for heavens sake, why didn't you tell us we needed these papers?"

Knowing it wasn't Nancy's fault, they were without the papers, Santa tried to soothe the matter over by saying, Donald, and you too Fred, will have to pay more attention to matters of this sort; after all, Nancy completed the forms and that was her part of the job. Your part was making certain you had them in your possession to be delivered.

61

Now, shall we go back and try again?" Hurrying back to the post office the three men, fortunately found the lines had shortened and they were promptly taken care of.

With all forms completed they went on their way to a stationery store to pick up the cardstock required by Leon and Phillip.

On the way home, Fred questioned Santa about who was going to service 'Santas Airways Group'?

Not quite understanding what Fred was thinking, Santa asked him to, "Define service when inquiring who is going to service the 'Santas Airways Group'?"

"Well," Fred explained, we are all gung-ho about hiring and training and giving people access to what we're developing, but where, after you have them trained are you going to place them? Will they be standing on street corners, in stores . . . where are you actually going to put them?"

Understanding what he was saying, though he was in agreement with him, it gave Santa something to think about. His thoughts were, 'All preparation and no place to go.'

"It looks as if I'll have to call another meeting," said Santa. "Your point is well taken Fred."

Reconsidering Santa proclaimed, "Rather than calling another meeting, since you've come right to the point, maybe this is the perfect project to be taken over by you and Donald. After all, if I were not in the picture, someone would have to work at completing what we've started; and it would be to your advantage to take over, since you already know what I am trying to do."

Immediately picking up on the convenience of the offer

placed before them, Donald told Santa, "You know that in the end, it's to our advantage to do the best we can, so to put you at ease, we will take on this project."

Being the clever manipulator he was, Donald continued proclaiming, "As long as we can consult with you and have your approval when we are handling matters properly, I cannot foresee any problem."

Listening to Donald make this point with Santa, Fred decided not to interrupt at this time, but to discuss it with Donald at a later date. This meant that Santa was turning over some reins.

Fred and Donald were really beginning to take an interest in the project Santa had given them. Until now, they had never been offered such an opportunity, and between them, they made a pact to stick it out to the end.

After their return to the house, they went back to the office regularly occupied by Leon, Phillip and Nancy. They were looking for quiet and privacy, to enable them to chart their plan of action. They found the paper and pencils they needed and started trying to list what it was they had in mind.

Fred asked Donald, "Now, what is it we are really trying to achieve?"

Thinking out loud, Donald said to Fred, "It seems to me as if we need a salesman."

Questioning Donald, Fred asked, "Why do we need a salesman? What do we have to sell?" and Donald's answer was, "Santas."

He continued to exploit the subject, saying, "We are advertising for Santas aren't we? Where are they going to work? What kind of work are they going to do?"

Fred seemed to be confused, but went on trying to help figure out a plan of action. "Well," he said, "if Santas are going to work, what is it they are going to do?"

Donald repeated the word, "Offer". . . over and over, "Offer . . . offer . . . offer. I know," he said, "they are going to offer a service. It's like, for instance; when a maid comes in to clean, she is offering a service for which she gets paid."

Then Fred said, "Who's going to pay these Santas and what kind of service are they going to perform?"

Donald repeated Fred's answer, "You are right; who's going to pay these Santas and what are they going to do?

Maybe we need some help from Santa with this project."

Fred suggested to Donald that they ask him after dinner if he would have time for a meeting with them tomorrow. We can tell him it's about the new project, and I'm certain he'll understand.

Suggesting they get their thoughts together so they would know exactly how to approach his mode of thinking, Donald answered, "That's a good thought Fred, but you know what I just remembered?"

What's that?" asked Fred.

Donald carefully replied, "We forgot to stop at the news office for the 'Help Wanted' applications we were suppose to bring back for Leon and Phillip. How about if we go for them now, so they'll be available for tomorrow?"

They went on their way to pick up the necessary forms, and returned home just in time for dinner. The children were also present, and Dorothy and Mary, who had been out galavanting around, had just come in, so Fred and Donald had no time to tell them what was happening.

Santa's Second Chance

Dinner was a gala affair with everyone discussing their activities of the day. Santa asked Bernard when school would be out for spring vacation, and he told him their break would start the end of the week.

Since this was Monday, it gave them only six more days for the work they had to do if they stayed through Sunday.

Santa told Margaret their trip was coming to an end. If they expected the trophy to be ready before their departure, they had better order it tomorrow.

Hearing of this decision, Fred asked Santa if he would have time for a meeting they needed to hold regarding procedure.

Being only too happy to hear the two men were taking their project seriously, Santa asked if a morning meeting would fit into their schedule and they assured him it would; they knew this meeting was important.

After dinner, Santa and Margaret going to their room, where they could talk privately, discussed a number of subjects he felt warranted her opinion. He also wanted her to know exactly what was happening.

"Margaret," Santa said, "there are so many ins and outs, and I want you to help me evaluate what I am doing. I think I have everything under control, and I have more confidence in Fred and Donald than I'm certain you know I've had in the past; they are like changed men.

Consequently, I gave them a new type of job, and I'm not even certain what to call it.

They've asked to have a meeting with me tomorrow, so I think it's safe to assume it is something important. Since I suggested the meeting take place in the A.M., you and I can go order the trophy in the afternoon. That should give the trophy shop a week to prepare it, and hopefully, deliver it before we are ready to leave.

By the way, the children will be out of school for spring break on Friday," added Santa. If we extend our stay until Monday, we will have plenty of time left to take care of business; so at breakfast, I'll let everyone know we will be departing on that day.

Meanwhile," Santa went on, "about the trophy. As you know, I definitely decided not to mention the names of the winners until we got back to Santa Land. Margaret, you'll never believe who captured first place. This was not because the ability to create a name wasn't there, but the rules of this contest strictly prohibited the family of committee members from participating in the program. It took a bit of deciphering and deduction, but I finally figured it out. I'm going to tell you Margaret, but this has to be our secret. We cannot utter a word, because I promised I would forget this ever happened.

However, I feel it's important for you to know, so you will be able to take a stand should the occasion ever arise.

Hon, can you even imagine who entered the name we are going to use?"

Looking puzzled, Margaret said to Santa, "My wildest imagination tells me it . . . could it have been Fred?"

It was then Margaret told him of Fred's antics with the theft of her belongings, before they were married; a topic in all of these years she had never before mentioned.

She continued saying, "But he seems to have overcome his problems, and as you remarked, Fred and Donald, both appear to be reformed men.

66

So there, now we both have secrets; but you still haven't told me your secret?"

Santa was definitely surprised by her expose' and then re-marked, "Well, there's no use crying over spilled milk, as long as we can clean up the mess."

Again Margaret said, "You haven't told me yet who your culprit is?"

As Santa hesitated, Margaret exclaimed, "Oh no . . . don't tell me it's Dorothy!"

Surprisingly, Santa asked, "Now how did you figure that one out?"

Margaret's answer was, "Let's just call it,

BIRDS OF A FEATHER

Irene Zulueta

ONE STEP AT A TIME

Voicing his opinion the next day when Santa, Fred and Donald met for their meeting, he told them, "I'm so glad to see you men are moving full speed ahead."

Fred interrupted what Santa was going to continue saying, by telling him that he and Donald had made a trip to the newspaper to pick up the forms Leon and Phillip needed which had been forgotten the previous day. "Realizing we might need them ourselves," he continued, "we decided to pick them up immediately and also to have this meeting with you."

Actually, because of his previous postal experience, Fred was trying to impress Santa with his ability to pay attention to the little matters that might crop up.

Santa was listening, but did not quite comprehend what Fred was trying to say. He complimented them on their decision to finish the task of returning for the applications; at the same time, in his mind, he questioned the need for this meeting.

Explaining the purpose of this meeting to Santa, Donald decided the best course to follow would be, telling tell him what he and Fred were trying to accomplish.

"When we talk about the hiring of men to play Santas, once you have them trained," asked Donald, "where are you going to use them?" Trying to approach the problem gently as well as tactfully, he continued by again asking Santa, "What do you think about hiring a salesman to sell a Santa's services, which are of course the services providing the need. . ."

Beginning to understand, Santa said, "You know, I think you are right. It looks like I haven't been thinking ahead. I'm so involved in trying to make this project work . . ." and as he hesitated, Fred decided to continue explaining their position.

"I think," Fred went on, "we need to hire a salesman or maybe one of us should go out and solicit perhaps . . . a toy store where a Santa might work; as a Santa of course, who would listen to children tell him what they would like to have brought to them as a Christmas surprise."

Having a bright idea Donald announced, "Maybe we should advertise that Santa is coming to town. Why don't we go to the local toy store and see if they would be willing to help us with this promotion. It undoubtedly could mean sales for them!"

"For instance," Fred continued, "if we went to the Toy Thrillers Store and offered your services Santa, simply to try it out, it would hopefully promote business for them, and it would give us an idea of how we need to train our Santas to go to work for their store . . . thus promoting sales! What do you think?"

Feeling very enthused about the whole idea Santa exclaimed, "Just imagine me as a Santa he thought, and then said, "But wait, I think I should change my name."

Donald quickly asked, "Why? There's nothing wrong with your name . . .!"

"Well," answered Santa, "I really don't want anyone to know who I am or that they can simply connect me to a gift-giving Santa . . ."

Coming up with a solution Fred added, "Well, how about if we just change the spelling of your last name from 'K' TO "C" and call you Santa Claus; and you will be the man in the store listening to the children tell you what they'd like to receive as a Christmas surprise!

Then you can ask them questions such as, have they been good or bad; what have they done to deserve this gift . . . oh, we could think up all kinds of questions and on the basis of these questions, we can train the men who apply for the job adequately and maybe, with a little bit of luck, you won't even have to pay them. Instead, let's just advertise for volunteers to play Santa Claus, to help establish our pilot program."

Santa listened intently, and then responded, "That's a superb solution! We'll have to get Leon and Phillip to work on it right away." Questioning Fred and Donald, Santa asked, "Is that what this meeting was about?"

Donald responded, "That was the biggest part of what we need . . ."

Without giving him a chance to continue Santa informed them, "It's time for Margaret and I to go order the trophy and pick up the prizes for the winners of the Naming Contest; how about continuing this meeting tomorrow, as I have to give this some real thought!"

They all agreed, and Santa went looking for Margaret.

After he left, Fred and Donald breathed a sigh of relief into excitement. They seem to have landed in Santa's good graces.

Donald said to Fred, "It looks as if we've finally done something right," and Fred followed up with, "Amen."

Santa and Margaret ventured out to order the trophy and prizes needed for the Naming Contest. They easily found the shop where trophies were on display and Santa knew exactly what he was going to have listed on the winner's trophy.

Feeling bad that he had to resort to this procedure, Santa as he entered the shop, dismissed the actual facts of the situation. All he could do was to look for an appropriate trophy, tell the clerk what he wanted engraved on it and when they needed delivery.

Finding a neat trophy bearing wings at its top that also had a plate where the first place name could be inscribed, he decided all he needed to add would be the creator's name, the date and year.

He hesitated because he knew how much this would mean to Dorothy, but he also knew it would help to prevent an argument between her and Fred; a confrontation whereas she might end up the loser, or so he was afraid.

Santa pulled out of his pocket a sheet of paper containing the listing to be engraved on the main plate. Margaret, standing by his side, had no idea what Santa was planning for the inscription.

She stepped aside and started to wander about the shop when all of a sudden, she spied an Afghan hound walking down the street, all alone. How unusual, thought Margaret, I wonder where the owner is.

She called back to Santa as she went out the door, "Hon, I'll be waiting for you outside."

As she stepped out the door, the Afghan seemed to sense her presence and came closer to where she stood. Reaching out to pet the hound, the dog responded by licking her hand. "How sweet," she said to herself, "I wonder to whom she belongs?"

Coming out of the shop to join her Margaret told Santa, "This poor dog is all alone. Evidently, she has become separated from her owner . . ." and she didn't give him a chance to answer her comment before she said, "Why don't we take her home with us? We could make some inquiries or advertise in the lost and found; perhaps her owner will come to claim her."

Santa agreed because, as usual, there was little he could refuse Margaret.

Needless to say, as they started on home, with a little bit of encouragement, the Afghan followed behind them in line, every step of the way. Margaret was secretly delighted.

Once they reached home, they found Mildred had prepared dinner and everyone was available. Dinner time was always a great event. The food was always scrumptiously delicious, the desserts were spectacular and the conversation was exhilarating; they all had something to contribute.

The children were looking forward to going home for their spring break; Leon, Phillip Nancy and Mildred were looking forward to the events of the festival, and even Fred, Dorothy, Mary and Donald seemed to miss Santa Land. In their minds, as different as it was, they concluded, 'There was no place like home'.

Finding no dog food in the cupboard, Margaret gathered all the leftover scraps from dinner and fed them to the Afghan, who ate contentedly.

Being overjoyed with the new dog, immediately after dinner Patrick groomed her to perfection and took her for a walk.

Margaret explained to Patrick, "She followed us home and we bonded almost immediately!"

Asking, "Aunt Margaret, are we going to take her home with

us?" Sadly she answered, "No Patrick, she's someone's pet, and as we sit here and talk about her, I'm sure they are missing this poor girl."

"How are we going to find her owner?" asked Patrick and Margaret answered, "First of all, we'll have to go down to the pound and check to see if anyone is looking for her; if not, we'll have to advertise in the 'Lost and Found'."

Feeling an attachment to the dog, Patrick asked, "Aunt Margaret, can we give her a name?" Her quick answer was, "Why not . . . what shall we call her?" With little hesitation Patrick said, "How about Mitzi?"

Looking surprised Margaret said, "For a dog of this stature, that's a great name.

Tomorrow," Margaret continued, "After you get home from school, we'll make a trip to the pound, and if no one is looking for her, we can go to the newspaper and place an ad in the 'Lost and Found'."

"I sure hope no one comes to claim her," remarked Patrick. Under her breadth Margaret said, "Me too!"

The next day, Patrick and Margaret found themselves at the pound with little result, so they proceeded to place a found advertisement in the newspaper. She assured Patrick, that placing an ad to find the owner was not only the right thing to do, it was all they could do.

Being anxious to hear what Santa had to say, Fred and Donald were ready for their next meeting.

One of the first comments turned to exploiting the appearance of a new Santa. He then said to the men, "You know, we're going to have to tear this project apart piece by piece to get satisfactory results."

"I understand what you are getting at Santa, but which is the first part to attack?" inquired Fred

Questioningly Santa asked, "How about if we attack age. Should we use this angle, and we are looking for volunteers, we will have to have men who most likely are no longer working, but at the same time we need men who can communicate with children."

Fred came up with, "You mean like men who are in their second childhood?"

Cringing at this answer Donald sarcastically said, "No, we mean men who drink milk instead of coffee!"

Playing out the scheme, Santa responded, "No . . ., I mean men who know how to interact with children and how to relate on most levels. In other words, they should know how to ask a childish question, but still, be able to handle the question like a man to a child."

Feeling embarrassed about his misconception Fred said, "That sounds more like it." Trying to recover from his remark he followed up with, "You guys know how I enjoy joking around."

"Now, if you can visualize this scene," Santa continued, "Here's how I see it!" He went on to describe the total picture.

"First," he said, "we will have to advertise as it gets closer to the Christmas season, that Santa Claus is coming to town. He will be appearing at, shall we say, 'The Toy Thrillers Store' for three weeks before Christmas, to take requests from children who would like to receive a Christmas Day Surprise.

Of course, reading this advertisement in the newspaper, parents will bring the children to the store to meet Santa, who they think is going to bring their Christmas gift. In reality, it will be the parents listening to the children's request who can purchase whatever they think they should have, or possibly, be able to afford. If it happens to be toys, they can buy it from the Toy Thrillers Store.

We will have to approach the store to present them with the idea and if it works, we can search out stores in other locations that might like to take part in the same plan. How does this sound so far?"

Acknowledging the plan as workable, Donald heard Fred ask Santa, "I thought you were going to be delivering those surprises on Christmas Eve?"

Stunned for a moment, Santa answered, "Well, yes I was but this approach seems to be a more practical solution. My participation would remain in delivering surprises to orphans and hospitals and shelters, places where there is no one to provide these niceties.

However, this is a part of the program we can work out later. For now, we have to organize the idea and take . . .

ONE STEP AT A TIME

Irene Zulueta

THREE MORE STEPS AT A TIME

With many intricate routes to be followed, Santa decided he'd better put some of these paths on paper. For instance, which endeavor was next in the way of priority? Maybe he should have a meeting with Leon and Phillip. They could certainly make a list of what had to be considered most important in view of the project.

Remembering, while he and Margaret had shopped for the first place trophy, they had forgotten to order the second, as well as runner-up prizes. Santa asked, "and where is Alex when I need him?" Reminding himself that Alex was busy in Santa Land preparing the grounds for a festival, he still needed someone to talk to and he looked for his best friend; who else but Margaret! Fortunately, she had just returned with Patrick and she was also looking for him.

Reporting the results of their trip to the pound, she secretly hoped like Patrick, if no owner was found, Santa might approve the idea of taking Mitzi back to Santa Land. Calling the dog Mitzi, he, inquired, "And who is Mitzi?"

Realizing she and Patrick had named the dog when Santa was not around, he would have no idea to whom the name Mitzi referred. After telling him, he was a bit disappointed to find there was no word of a lost dog owner, because he knew exactly what Margaret was thinking; another dog in Santa Land was definitely not what they needed. And yet. . ., Margaret asked for so little, he knew if no owner showed up, they would have to bring Mitzi back with them.

I can't worry about that now, he thought to himself, I have other matters that need taking care of, and he told Margaret, "I'm going to look for Leon and Phillip. I need some input about their plans and progress."

Trying to catch up with them, he found Leon and Phillip fast at work, mostly on advertising, both for the newspaper and also signs for the festival. When they told him about the progress they were making, he was happy to find them, once again, so steadfast in their preparation.

Santa again wondered if he was biting off more than he could chew. Then he remembered, it was he who would always tell Alex he had to take . . . one step at a time!

Next he went to his desk where he felt he could gather his thoughts, thus enabling him to make a decent presentation to the rest of the crew. As he looked at the empty paper in front of him, he picked up his pencil and titled the first page, 'SANTAS AIR-WAYS GROUP'. Next he wrote, 'REQUIREMENTS'. Then on the outline came 'PURPOSE'. He seemed puzzled . . . about which came first, the hiring of applicants or locations in which to place them.

Answering his own question, he saw that they needed a salesman first, because if they had no store in which to work, they didn't need to do any recruiting. Talking to himself, Santa commented, "Maybe my logic is back in operation. The next question is who . . . ?"

At once picturing Fred, since he finally seemed to under-stand the project and because Donald was the first to mention the hiring of a salesman, he thought, let them work it out while we're within range of a toy store. With this idea in mind, Santa looked for Fred and Donald so they could discuss the situation.

Looking in the barn and back in the house, he finally found them at the conference table. Inviting himself to join them he asked, "If I can disturb you fellows for a few minutes, we need to have a discussion, and I would like some help."

Fred and Donald were all ears as Santa pulled up a chair and sat down, indicating he was ready to talk. Donald asked, "What's up Santa?"

Aggressively, he said, "Fred and Donald, you were right when you mentioned hiring a salesman. If you will, I would like you to visit the Toy Thrillers Store and introduce our program to them. If they will agree to our promotion, I'll come back at Christmas time and play Santa Claus free of charge, so we can learn if this idea is feasible. After we find it works, we can hire a salesman to go into other parts of the country to sell this same promotion. In this manner, we will not have to spend money hiring a salesman we can't afford."

Speaking up Donald said to Fred encouragingly, "Fred, I know you'll make a great salesman, and if you'd like, I'll go along with you."

Fred's gulp could be heard throughout the room and though hesitancy prodded his being, he did not want to disappoint Santa and uttered, "Well Santa, I think we are on to something . . . something big. Tell me, how many more days before we return to Santa Land?"

Telling them he expected to leave on Monday in the early A.M., Santa suggested the return could be extended by a day or two if it would help!

Doing the calculation in his head Fred said, "We need a little preparation for this job; Donald and I will explore the avenues we can travel, and if you will extend our stay as you mentioned," and he threw in, "'weather permitting,'" it would be helpful. That will give us time to prepare and we'll go to the Toy Thrillers Store on Monday."

Tilting his head to one side, Santa then agreed saying, "I don't see why not, so I'll tell everyone at dinner, we will be leaving in a few days. That will give them extra time for frivolities, and it will give us a chance to continue on with opportunity, even if only one step-at-a-time. With this concrete decision, Santa left to take his regular nap.

Wasting no time, Fred and Donald sat down to begin an analyzation of the position in which Santa had placed them, along with their preparation for a trip to the Toy Thrillers Store. Looking at one another Fred asked, "Where do we begin, Donald?"

Having some ideas of his own, Donald wasn't quite certain how to tell Fred that he needed to spruce up his appearance. "Haircuts for both of us might be in order . . .," suggested Donald. He went on intimating, "If we are going to . . . that is if you are going to be a salesman, you'll have to look successful."

Taking the comment constructively Fred added, "Why don't we ask the girls to give us haircuts?"

Before doing anymore planning, they went looking for Mary and Dorothy to tell them what was happening, but they were evidently once again, out galavanting around; however, they did manage to locate Margaret.

Speaking first Fred asked her outright, "Can you cut hair, Margaret?"

Looking at them weirdly she inquired, "What kind of hair Fred?"

Speaking up for both of them Donald replied, "Fred and I need haircuts so we can take on the appearance of successful salesmen when we go to the Toy Thrillers Store, as Santa suggested."

Not having heard of Santa's latest diversion, she had no idea what he was planning, but then she remembered, she'd heard Alfonso had a talent for cutting hair so she recommended they talk to him, as she could be of little help.

Rushing out to look for Alfonso, they found him and presented their problem; he was happy to accommodate them.

Dressing the part the two men considered, was their next step. Looking at the clothing they'd brought with them, they decided nothing in their wardrobe looked impressive, so back to Margaret they went and asked her what she thought.

Being quite resourceful, Margaret pictured the velvet, charcoal grey drapes adorning the windows in one of the rooms of the house; she anticipated there being enough material in the drapes to make two pair of trousers and possibly two vests, but not enough for jackets. Next she thought to herself, I brought along an extra petticoat, and out of this, they should be able to get two fancy shirts.

"Now," she said, "you'll have to talk to Alfonso again, because he, I understand, also has tailoring experience and I do believe there's a sewing machine in the cellar that he might be able to crank up to do a decent job."

Hurrying back to Alfonso once again, Donald and Fred asked for his help.

Getting along with the men quite favorably, Alfonso already knew the problems facing them so he agreed to tailor their suits; besides, he knew how much this project meant to Santa.

The three of them found the room containing the drapes, and Fred with Donald helped remove them from the windows. Next they went to the cellar to retrieve the sewing machine which had been left behind when they moved.

Having finished tailoring their new clothes, Alfonso thought the two men, sporting stylish haircuts, were the picture of dapper gentlemen; that was, until one looked at their feet. Now what, they thought! How would they solve this problem? What were they going to do about their shoes? Polish would not be sufficient to make their shoes look as if they went with their outfits.

Fred asked Donald, "Buddy, do you have any money on you?" Donald's quick response was, "No! Do you?"

While discussing the relevant problem, Margaret came along and noticed how spry they appeared and she looked at them, up and down; but the shoes they were wearing stuck out like a sore thumb. Immediately recognizing the problem, and knowing they had no resource for money, she dug deep into the pocket of her apron, pulled out some cash and divided it in two; handing the money to the men, she told them, "This is between you and me . . . there is no need for anyone else to know. Several blocks from here, is a thrift store; the kind that relieves wealthy people of their unwanted items. If you hurry down there, you may find some wonderful bargains that will help you look like the successful salesmen I know you are going to be, as well as, providing something that will match your new outfits. Now, Go!"

The men hurried to the Thrift Store and as luck would have it, found exactly what they needed, with cash left to spare.

This was definitely what one called, taking . . .

THREE MORE STEPS AT A TIME

Irene Zulueta

A NEW HOLIDAY

All of the maneuvering had to be accomplished in one day; this meant that Fred and Donald had one more day for preparation of whatever. The following day, they continued their discussion of trying to evaluate the process of selling their promotion.

First they asked questions like:

1. Who do we contact?   Then,

2. What's the purpose for this promotion? Next

3. What does the store have to gain?   Finally

4. What does the customer have to gain?

Fred and Donald had an answer for each question as they went along.

Deciding to contact the manager, who in this case having already made an inquiry, found his name to be Mr. Tankeroo. They concentrated on the answer to question number two; the purpose for the promotion; deciding it was to help fulfill children's dreams about the real reason for Christmas. They went on to question number three, what does the store have to gain? The answer to this one was publicity as well as profit from increased sales.

For the customer and question number four; entertainment for the adults and children free of charge, along with shopping satisfaction.

They would explain that for the trial promotion Santa Claus

would appear in the store, at no cost.

Donald and Fred decided that no more questions needing answers were necessary. If they had failed to think of anything, they would have to play it by ear; and they both thought of themselves as clever enough to devise an intelligent answer.

When the next morning came, they rose, had breakfast and quickly dressed. When they finished, they once again looked, like very dapper salesmen.

Before going out the door, they discussed their plan of action. Realizing they had not asked Santa for the dates on which he would be available to actually offer his services as Santa Claus, they also had to know who would pay the advertising bill for this promotion.

Looking for him, before taking leave, they found Santa in the barn attending his fleet.

"Santa," asked Fred, "we need to know when you will return to play Santa Claus? After all, this is only April and . . ."

Understanding the problem, Santa immediately answered, "How about July . . .? As a special promotion we can call it 'Christmas in July.'"

As for the advertising, the store can feature this as a special promotion and since they already advertise on a regular basis, we can tell them we'll have an advertisement drawn up by our executives free of charge. All they will have to do is place the ad in the paper to announce, Santa Claus is coming to town for a 'Special Promotion' which will take place on . . . let's say, a weekend at the beginning of July, and then announce that Santa will also return at Christmas time.

Before we make any further plans, we had better inquire

whether or not the Toy Thriller Store will work with us. Good Luck, fellas!" and Santa walked out of the barn leaving Fred and Donald astonished, but satisfied that he thought they could handle the situation, as it was now or never.

Fred and Donald checked their appearances one more time before leaving the house and as they peered into a full length mirror they caught a glimpse of Mary and Dorothy watching in the background. As they turned, Mary remarked to Donald, "Sir, can I help you?"

Knowing she was talking to him, Donald said, "Oh Mary, don't be so funny . . ." and she then replied, "Oh Donald, for a moment I didn't recognize you. You are the man I married, aren't you?"

Donald answered, "Mary, Love . . . , when we wed, I didn't have a new fashionable haircut, or even a suit as fine. It kind of makes me feel as if I'm living in the lap of luxury."

While Dorothy was waiting to get her word in, Fred asked, "How do you like it Dorothy? Do you think I'll pass as a successful salesman?"

"Honey," remarked Dorothy, "I'd buy anything you were selling! Just try me." Fred retorted, "How much money do you have?" Dorothy hemmed and answered, "Well, actually I don't have any."

Fred uttered, "Sorry, no deal. I'll have to take my talent elsewhere," and with these words he and Donald proceeded to leave the house with Mary and Dorothy wishing them luck in their venture.

The two men sauntered down the street, until they could see the Toy Thriller Store sign. It was an elegant sign, made special and to order, projecting a picture of prosperity.

Santa's Second Chance

As Fred and Donald entered the front door, they encountered the cashier, but the store was unoccupied; there was not a customer in sight.

Fred, being the salesman he thought he was, asked the cashier, "May I see your manager, Mr. Tankeroo?"

Responding the cashier asked, "And what is your business sir?"

With knees shaking, Fred looked at Donald while answering, "A Sales Promotion ma'am which we are launching; should he like the idea and want to become involved, we feel the promotion will bring in customers as well as business. However, first we must explain the procedure which will take place and how it operates."

The cashier deciding she would make Mr. Tankeroo's decision for him answered forcefully, "No Mr. Tankeroo is not seeing anyone today; you'll have to come back at another time."

Donald found the substance to cut in with, "But ma'am, we are from out of town . . . , we are leaving to return home in a few days, and the last toy store on which we have to call is way on the other side of town. If Mr. Tankeroo can't be seen today, we may have to make this offer to your competitor and . . ."

As Donald was finishing his statement, a door leading to the back room opened. Out stepped a stately gentleman asking the cashier if everything was okay.

He'd heard the last words Donald had pronounced, "to make this offer to your competitor . . .," and he said, I didn't hear the first part of the sentence and I would like to know what you are going to offer my competitor . . . is it something about which I should be concerned?"

Assuming it was Mr. Tankeroo, Fred took over and asked the gentleman's name. When he heard the man tell them he was Mr. Tankeroo, General Manager of the Toy Thrillers Store, Fred responded, "Oh Mr. Tankeroo, I'm pleased to meet you. Your lovely cashier was getting ready to arrange a meeting between us, so we could offer you the chance of a lifetime promotion. We had mentioned that our time before returning home was short and we might have to eliminate your competition across town."

At the sound of the word 'competition', Mr. Tankeroo said to them, "Why don't you gentlemen follow me into my office! I'd like to hear more about this promotion."

As Fred and Donald followed Mr. Tankeroo, their faces filled with joy. Sitting opposite him they explained the whole procedure.

Basically, Mr. Tankeroo was a gambler and business at the time was nothing to write home about, so in his mind what did he have to lose?

Upon getting ready to leave the store, Donald and Fred shook hands with Mr. Tankeroo, while telling him, he would hear from them in the next few months when they returned to town. They also assured him he would not be unhappy with the decision he'd just made.

Ignoring the fact that she was a belligerent cashier, they thanked her for the effort expended and the two went on their way.

They could hardly wait to tell Santa of their success. Reaching home in due time, they found him in the midst of playing a game of Chinese Checkers with Edward and Bernard; Santa was winning and the game was almost over.

Anxiously awaiting to hear the outcome of the meeting he

stood up from the table on which they were playing and accidentally tipped the checkerboard as he removed himself from the chair; marbles went flying in every direction. Santa said to the two boys, "Sorry fellas! Remind me to have Alex make up a new board for you; one that can be played with pegs instead of marbles."

Then Santa turned to Fred and Donald standing in front of the fireplace, and asked, "Well guys, were you successful?"

Hardly being able to contain himself, Fred knowing with the help of Donald, he'd achieved his first concrete sale, or so to speak. He could now consider himself a bonafide salesman.

Hearing the news, Santa was totally exalted. Little did he know this was the beginning of a new holiday, soon to be called 'CHRISTMAS'.

Fred looked at a calendar and remarked to Donald, "We're right on schedule, with mission accomplished. Now it's back to Santa Land for fun and games.

They delivered the good news to Leon and Phillip and then went off to see if Margaret needed any help. Having located her, they told her of their accomplishment and she was thrilled with the progress they'd made. Having inquired about her needing any help, Fred and Donald knew their embarkation date was the next day, early in the morning, weather permitting.

Margaret asked them to put the prizes for the Naming Contest, along with other items purchased for the festival into the cart.

Mentioning ever so slightly, she thought they should leave their new clothes behind at the house for future use. Looking so handsome wearing them, Margaret knew they would want to be donning them all the time; she also knew the drapes from other windows in the house could not be removed to make new clothes.

Fred and Donald understood Margaret's suggestion and were totally committed to cooperation. Loading everything necessary to take with them for their return they then sought Mary and Dorothy to make certain everyone's bags were packed, and also to deliver the news of their success in selling the promotion.

Wanting to please Margaret, Santa gave in to the idea of taking Mitzi back to Santa Land; to date no one had claimed her and Margaret refused to return her to the pound. Considering no one would be available in Ireland to care for her, Santa felt he had no alternative but to give in; consequently Fred and Donald secured Mitzi in the sleigh, along with Patricks's two cats, Rascal and Tyrant, in the cart.

In essence, that meant they would be returning to Ireland in the midst of summer, but for now, it was time for their flight back to Santa Land to prepare for not only a festival, but also . . .

A NEW HOLIDAY

MATCH MADE IN HEAVEN

The return flight to Santa Land seemed especially smooth, with a heavenly atmosphere prevailing as everyone vacated the sleigh.

The complicated work of the festival was quickly approaching and Alex was right on hand to show Santa and Margaret what he'd accomplished in their absence; all they needed to finish would be the complete coordination of the programs as they were to occur.

Being anxious to know who had won the Naming Contest, he thought it best to wait for Santa to reveal the winner when he was ready.

Leon, Phillip, Nancy and Mildred were happy to renew acquaintances with comrades they had missed during their stay in Ireland.

There were many aspects to which they compared their previous life in Santa Land; the only problem was being unable to decide where they felt more comfortable.

Alfonso, Alfred and Alex had already settled into their new living quarters on the second floor of the post office.

When Santa and Margaret viewed the Conference Room, they loved the beautiful woodwork adorning the completed room. Even the benches for the elves were in place; should there be a need for them in view of an oncoming meeting.

Having checked out the new barn, Santa and Margaret

moved on to look over the arrangement Alex had provided for the grounds behind the castle where the festival was to be held. Like the post office, and everything else he had built, the grounds were truly beautiful. The concrete foundations laid behind the castle were perfect for setting up the three tents they needed for the festivities, along with the slab of cement to be used as a stage.

"This Alex," Santa murmured to himself, "always seems to know exactly what he is doing. His interpretations of what we need are always so accurate."

Then he remembered the office he relegated in the castle as a surprise for Margaret, but he needed to talk to Alex first before telling her about it.

Having completed their observations, Santa asked Margaret if she had given any thought to a date for the festival.

Answering him as specifically as she could, Margaret replied, "Well, I think we should hold it as soon as we can; after all, if you are going back to play Santa in July, Leon and Phillip won't have too much time, depending on the outcome, to prepare the real Christmas advertising."

"Hon, you are assuming everything is going to go well . . . that all will be acceptable and our project will be a success . . ." then stopping to think Santa continued, "What if this idea doesn't work . . ., then what?"

Having faith in Santa, Margaret encouraged him with, "Don't be a doubting Thomas, we'll cross that bridge when we come to it."

Trying to decide on a date for the affair, Margaret suggested, "Hon, why don't you call a meeting to check out how ready everyone is for this event, and then we can also explain to them the necessity of time regarding your trip to play Santa Claus in July.

Meanwhile, I'll introduce Mitzi to Snapper and Mewpurr, and make room for her . . . or, how about moving the two of them from the kitchen to the new barn with the rest of the animals?"

Hearing this suggestion gave Santa a sense of relief since the kitchen was already crowded with just Mewpurr and Snapper.

Telling Santa there was a stall in the new barn that would easily accommodate the two dogs, Margaret proceeded to take Mitzi to the location that would be her new home. Next, she would bring Snapper out to finalize the arrangement between them.

"Maybe we could temporarily leave Mewpurr where she is," commented Margaret, so she will have no hard feelings about the addition of another dog. You know how fond Mewpurr is of Snapper. I just hope Snapper becomes as fond of Mitzi as he is of Mewpurr."

After showing Mitzi her new home, Margaret thoughtfully returned to the kitchen and attempted to pick up Snapper's pillow bed. Thinking she was playing with him, he grabbed the pillow from the opposite end to prevent Margaret from taking it. Having finally retrieved the pillow, she glanced back to see Mewpurr alongside Snapper with a comforting look, as well as a question on their faces, as if to ask, "What's going on?"

Stopping to pick up a leash, Margaret placed it around Snapper's neck and urged him to follow her, which he did leaving Mewpurr behind. As they approached the barn, Margaret announced to Snapper, "Sweetheart, I have a surprise for you . . ." and in Snapper's mind appeared the words 'What now'!

91

Approaching the stall in which she'd left Mitzi, Margaret told him, "I hope you like this Snapper . . . I've brought you a new friend."

Wagging his tail ferociously, Snapper looked straight ahead into the eyes of what he thought was the most beautiful friend to which anyone could have introduced him. She's even prettier than Mewpurr, he thought. Evidently, he'd never thought of Mewpurr as a different species from himself.

Removing Snapper's leash, Margaret allowed him to advance forward to where Mitzi was standing and at once as he reached her, he began to lick her face ever so gently! All Margaret could think when she saw Snapper's affectionate nature on display, was the report she'd give Santa about this match.

Having solved one problem, Margaret returned to the house to work on her next priority.

Finding Santa waiting for her, Margaret described the introductory scene featuring Mitzi and Snapper as they met in the barn. She was so thrilled about the new relationship Santa could feel the happiness of her beating heart with his joining in the rhythm.

Consequently, thinking this was a good time to tell her about the office she could call her own, Santa asked Margaret to come with him so she could approve his idea about a space he wanted to renovate; but still being careful not to say it was his surprise for her.

Being happy to oblige him, Margaret followed along as they returned to an empty room in the castle, close to the storeroom where they placed all the unused and newly purchased merchandise for safekeeping.

Before they could go into the storeroom, they had to pass

through an empty room. Not being as large as the office near the Conference Room in the post office, the dimensions were considerably larger than Santa's office.

Looking at Santa, Margaret asked, "And what do you propose we do with this area?"

Speaking seriously, Santa explained, "Hon, I thought you might like to have this room made into an office for yourself so you wouldn't have to spend all of your time in the kitchen."

Thoughtfully, she responded, "But this room is so big . . . what would I do with all of this space?"

Responding to her question, Santa commented, "When we arrange the furniture, it won't be as big as it looks."

Wanting to think about it, she didn't refuse his offer, because she was envisioning a different picture and suggested, "Why don't you take this space and I'll take your office. In that way you will be in a much easier to reach position and I certainly don't mind being upstairs. All we will have to do is move the furniture from your room into this one, and I'll see what we can do to fix up your office for me." Knowing there was still furniture left at the house in Ireland, Margaret thought she could have it brought back to Santa Land on their next trip.

Replying to her suggestion, Santa immediately recognized the value of her offer and while in the process of agreeing with her asked, "Do you really think you would be happy with that room?"

Speaking affirmatively Margaret responded, "Sweetheart, if your office is big enough for you, it is certainly big enough for me; and besides, you would be able to protect the storeroom so anyone wanting to get in there would have to go through your office first."

Questioning her thoughts, Santa asked, "Now who would want to get in there . . . besides, there is a door at the other end; one does not have to go through my office to get into the store-room, and yet . . . I suppose it's worth thinking about . . . especially with the possibility of holding a training school for Santas at this location . . . one never knows who or what we will find, even among the most honorable of men!

Yes, I will replace my office with this one, and you can have the space upstairs. I'll set the wheels in motion Margaret, and I think, positively speaking we have another . . .

MATCH MADE IN HEAVEN"

THE OFFICE OF

MARGARET KLAUS

Finding Alex was the next chore for Santa and he found him doing a production check in the workshop.

Feeling content about the new decisions which prevailed, Margaret went directly to Santa's old office with the purpose of trying to figure out a furniture arrangement that would suit her after he removed the present items.

Trying to remember what was left at the house in Ireland, Margaret pictured two of her favorite chairs, as well as another easy chair in which she once curled up to take short naps while caring for her parents when they were ill.

Remembering the furniture Fred had stored in the basement, she thought a desk had been left behind that would just suit this office.

While thinking about the furniture to be brought back on their next trip she realized, the children would be going back to school at the end of their spring break meaning the end of this week.

Donald and Fred could take the cart along on their return and come back with the necessary items. Also, they would have to hold the festival almost at once.

Margaret knew she had better find Santa and give him the new timetable regarding the festival, and the reason it should be held almost immediately. She knew the children might possibly miss one or two days of school but any more than that would be unthinkable.

Discussing plans about his new office, Santa and Alex saw Margaret come through the door. They knew something important was brewing.

Quickly dispensing the words, "Greetings Margaret," Santa then asked, "What's up my Dear?"

Hardly being able to contain her concern, Margaret blurted out, "Hon, if everyone is ready, we'll have to hold the festival, right away. I don't think anyone realized the children have to be back in school this coming week. I imagine it wouldn't hurt to let them miss a day or two, but no more."

Hearing of this predicament, Santa totally agreed and asked Alex, "Do you think you can get everyone together for a meeting tomorrow?"

Knowing the importance of the situation he responded, "Let's plan on it . . . first thing in the morning . . . and shall I tell them in the Conference Room?"

"You've got it!" replied Santa.

Happy that the subject was taken care of, Margaret added, "One other thing Hon, when Fred and Donald take the children back to school, they should also take the cart because there is furniture which needs to be brought back with them on their return."

Explaining her new ideas regarding the office furniture needed, Santa decided they should make the trip themselves; along with Fred, Donald, the children and anyone who needed to return to Ireland. They would take his reindeer and cart rather than Donald's and Fred's.

Then, Santa turned to Alex and asked, "For a change, would

you like to come along." Feeling flattered, Alex accepted his offer and it seemed as if everything was decided.

The next step would be tomorrow's meeting.

As the time for the meeting approached, Alex was busy rearranging the setup of the Conference Room for his comrades as well as, for Donald and Fred with their wives.

This time, Margaret made a point of attending so she could hear first hand what was going to take place.

Santa sat at the new conference table along with Margaret on one side and Alex on the other. Next to Alex were Mary and Donald, while Fred and Dorothy sat on Margaret's side. Included at the table were Leon, Phillip, Alfred, Alfonso and Nancy as part of the committee and Vivian, the new secretary for Santa Land.

The balance of their comrades became the audience, anxiously waiting to hear who had won the Naming Contest and what the new name for 'Santa Klaus Anonymous' was going to be.

The time to begin the meeting was at hand and standing up, Santa began with his greeting.

"I want to thank you for your attendance on such short notice, but as you will hear, time is fleeting. As I said when I originally made the announcement about the festival, it was to take place when we returned from Ireland.

While we've usually been able to overcome obstacles, a problem has arisen which we did not anticipate. I'm not saying we cannot overcome it, but it demands immediate action on everyone's part. Now tell me, how many of you are ready for the festival if we hold it in three days?" The absolute show of hands at 100% meant total cooperation putting Santa at ease.

He went on to say . . . "Thank you . . . I knew I could count on you." Next on this agenda . . ." Santa added, "Having taken the Naming Contest into consideration after studying all of your entries, we have three winners which we will disclose at the festival. In two days, we will pass out a program that will give you the line up for the events taking place.

The parade will start at the workshop and head down to the street leading onto the festival grounds behind the castle.

That you might know the reason we are holding the festival so quickly" he added, "the children have to return to school at the beginning of next week; even more important is getting ready for my return to Ireland to play Santa Claus in July.

Given a bit more time, we may be able to come up with something even more challenging for those of you who are talented enough to perform in an exhibition at the same time. If we are able to manage a show of this nature, I'll give you plenty of advance notice!

At this time, unless you have questions, I have no more to report, the meeting is concluded."

As the elves left the Conference Room, Dorothy asked "Are Mary and I going to be able to go this time, or do we have to stay home again?"

Trying to take the pressure from Santa having to give her a negative response, Margaret injected, "Dorothy, I thought we might take this opportunity to have our own meeting while the men are away so we can get back to what I originally had in mind.?"

Knowing this is what they'd been waiting for, Mary contributed to her answer, "We just got home Dorothy it's time to sit back and relax. It isn't often we can enjoy the peace and quiet, without having to face the responsibility of cooking . . . dishes . . . not to mention laundry. . . "

"Besides," Santa added, "It will practically be an overnight trip! I'm only going to help with the furniture that needs to be brought back to Santa Land."

Santa's last remark ended the inquisitive conversation and the room emptied, leaving only he, Alex and Margaret.

Realizing what she had promoted, Margaret declared, "It looks as if I'm going to have to make good on my decision; but if I work on my proposal in your old office, I'm going to need at least a table and several chairs until you return from Ireland with the furniture."

Knowing Santa would ask Alex to bring the table and chairs to her new office, Margaret suggested they all help remove what was left down to his recent acquisition before taking the necessary items to her current space.

Learning of the transition to take place, Alex immediately put his crew to work making a plaque to be placed over the door which read, "The Office of Margaret Klaus."

Seeing this engraved mounting overhead pleased Margaret to no end.

It wasn't long before Alex had Jake and Jeffry arranging the available table and chairs to her liking.

She'd brought along a few pads of paper for her and the girls, ink for writing and a lantern to shed some light on the subjects she would discuss with Mary and Dorothy; but for now, it was time to work on the festival.

Once again, she drew up a list of the events taking place on Saturday. It occurred to her, that she needed more than a list; she needed some contact with the children who had not been included or even invited to the morning meeting. That meant she would have to talk to Jayne, and Rex, Jean, Joan and Gerald, as well as Vivian who would be producing the program Santa had promised the participants in a couple of days.

Leaving her office, Margaret went to look for Jayne, who she felt certain would give her a helping hand, as she was capable of the communication necessary with the rest of the participants in their chosen categories.

Reaching the Gilpatrick's and O'Hare's apartment she learned Jayne was probably with the others practicing their gymnastics routine. Margaret left word to have Jayne come by Santa's old office, as she needed to speak with her.

At the same time, thinking ahead, as she always tried to do, Margaret decided to look for Nancy; she was certain in the short time left for revisions on the program to be drawn up, she would be a big help.

Finding Nancy visiting with Dolores, she told her she needed some assistance and they returned to Margaret's office. On the way, she told Nancy just why she needed help and what had to be done.

Concluding that the aid she needed involved someone, in addition to Alex, who could communicate with the elves, Margaret said, "While I know you are going back to Ireland, this is just a one time occurrence to get the festivities into proper prospective in time for Saturday.

By the time they reached Margaret's office, Nancy graciously agreed, she would be only too happy to help. As they sat down at the table, Margaret handed Nancy a list of the events that were to take place on Saturday. With both looking at her list, Margaret said, "I figure the parade should start at 10:00; everyone should be up and out by that time.

First in order is the Parade of Clowns in which Alex will appear, not as a clown but as a Grand Marshal; next will be the Animal Parade, conducted by Patrick, Ralph and Jake, as the animals will lead everyone to the grounds behind the castle. I think it would be well to hold the Gymnastics Show before the Talent Show . . ., and she asked, "What do you think Nancy?"

Feeling Margaret had everything under control, she agreed with her interpretation, but added, "If you hold the Barbeque before the Talent Show . . . everyone will be able to sit back and eat while enjoying the entertainment. Maybe the races should come before the barbeque because everybody will most likely, have eaten too much to be able to do any racing."

"Point well taken!" answered Margaret.

Then Nancy commented, "If you let them wander around, after the Animal Parade, they can enjoy the Cake Walk, the Dart Games, the Fortune Teller/Palm Reader and they can go to the Bakery Booth for their dessert, which they can eat after the Talent Show, while waiting for the announcement of the winners of the Naming Contest."

Appreciating Nancy's help, Margaret then gave her a list of names connected with each event and Nancy agreed to contact them individually to confirm their involvement on anything related to the festival.

A knock on the door brought Jayne into Margaret's office as Nancy was taking leave to begin fulfilling her helpful duties. Covering subjects with Jayne, Margaret asked about the Gymnastics Show, who would be performing in the Talent Show and what kind of races they have lined up for her friends.

After filling in the detail for Margaret, she asked Jayne to get in touch with Nancy so she would know who among her comrades to contact regarding the various activities.

Realizing this was a good idea, a feeling of importance settled within Jayne. Without a doubt she had evidently been taken into Aunt Margaret's confidence for this important occasion.

Producing the festival in two days caused energy and action to take precedence in the way of preparation throughout the village.

Having forwarded the information needed to help Vivian prepare the Events Program, Nancy decided to look for Jayne at the same time Jayne was looking for her.

Finding one another, Jayne was anxious to tell Nancy of her accomplishment and consequently reported, "I've gone over all these items with Aunt Margaret and she requested that I cover them with you, so you can pass them on to Vivian.

First of all, we have the names of the racers and then, the participants in the Gymnastics Show. Aunt Margaret suggested the barbeque take place before the Talent Show."

Listening to Jayne, Nancy realized, this little entrepreneur in her mind, was running the whole show. Well why not she thought, she had to learn the angles sometime . . . now is as good a time as any while she's on her own turf.

Consequently, she agreed with everything Jayne had to say because she knew Vivian would produce the program within the realms of extended borders as well as what was essential. The most important items were the names of performers and Jayne had jotted them all on paper so Nancy could communicate with them regarding their performances.

Sheila was to sing a solo, while Holly was a tap dancer with her own special routine. Bronson playing the guitar, along with Jessica, allowed the two to perform a duet. Ralph sang as a tenor would, and Meagan also sang as a soprano could. Often they would sing together, but this time they would sing individually; maybe someday they too would become a duet. Exceptional as a crooner, everyone dearly loved Frank. That made seven entrants in the Talent Show.

Then Jayne introduced a thought she had about the awards, to be given to the contestants appearing in the Talent Show. She whispered it into Nancy's ear hoping no one could hear, (as if anyone could) what she felt was appropriate placements for the winning artists.

Surprised at her suggestion, Nancy immediately agreed and Jayne felt content with her overwhelming willingness to accept this idea.

Leaving Nancy, Jayne bid her farewell and called back, "If you need me for anything, I'll be around." Going on her way, Jayne again glanced at the plaque bearing the name of Margaret Klaus. She knew one day, the name over the door would read Jayne Gilpatrick instead of . . .

THE OFFICE OF MARGARET KLAUS

Irene Zulueta

THE ENTERTAINING ELVESTOS

Having completed the programs together, Nancy and Vivian had them ready to be passed out the next day. There was only one day left for everyone to put their acts together as Saturday was Festival Day.

Santa and Margaret went into the storeroom to check all the prizes they purchased as awards in Ireland. The fruit baskets would be fresh, and the sausages were gathered for the winners in the races.

Mildred, Margaret and the others would bring out their elegant baked goods not only for the cakewalk, but also for dessert.

The meat was set out to thaw and made ready for barbequing.

Santa set out the dart games, while Alex with available comrades, set up three tents along with bleachers and picnic tables.

Margaret brought out the glass balls for the Fortune Teller; for the Palm Reading, Gypsy would have to operate on her own.

There was an array of prizes available for each performer in the Gymnastics Show, along with titles of Honorable Mention.

So far, so good . . . it looked as though everything was covered with the exception of the 'Naming Contest'! Santa kept the trophy for the 'Naming Contest' covered with a blanket; it would be the last item to be placed within view of the crowd.

Santa's Second Chance

The evening passed quickly and Festival Day promptly arose with everyone ready and waiting to start the parade. First came the clowns and next came the sleigh drawn by the animals, carrying Alex as the Grand Marshal. Once they were returned to their places in the barn everyone wandered around, taking advantage of the amusements at hand.

Races were quickly run and it wasn't long before the Gymnastics Show was ready to erupt. Everyone found seats in the bleachers that Alex had set up for them. To those who had never seen a Gymnastics Show, smiles and applause showed their appreciation for the effort expended.

With the show at an end, everyone headed toward the barbeque and picnic tables. This gave them the opportunity of sitting and listening to the performers of the Talent Show while devouring their delicious treats.

Taking their places on stage, one by one, the contestants performed their hearts out. The audiences clapped wildly with an unbridled enthusiasm, and this helped Santa to know his efforts had paid off.

Calling Jayne forward to present the awards for the Talent Show, even Santa was surprised when he heard her announce a seven way tie for first place.

While some were still busy consuming their desserts, Santa took center stage and called out, "Is everyone happy?" Hearing the unanimous response, Margaret joined him on stage, thus giving him a kiss on his cheek. Delighting in her action the crowd applauded to no end. There was no telling how far they would go for such an ideal and compatible couple.

Continuing, while anticipating what to expect, Santa moved closer to the trophy still covered and surrounded by beautifully wrapped fruit baskets on each side.

Santa called out loudly, "I know you are all anxious to hear the name we will assume to replace 'Santa Klaus Anonymous'. For now, I am going to announce the second runner up and . . . while this is equivalent to Third Place, I want to thank Andrew for his submission of Santa's Air Reserve. Andrew, will you join us on stage!" Waiting for Andrew to arrive, Santa went on to name the Second Place Winner, or first runner up.

"Belonging to Gypsy, who submitted, 'The Flying Santas'," he continued, "If Gypsy saw this name in her glass ball, it's a good thing she picked it out and entered it in our Naming Contest, as it has become our Second Place winner. Gypsy, will you come for your award."

Knowing first place would prove to be an awkward situation, Santa continued to move toward the trophy so he could remove the cloth that covered it as he spoke. Being uncertain which to do first, remove the wrap or announce the name, he started by placing his hand on the covering while shouting loudly, "The name we have adopted to replace 'Santa Klaus Anonymous' and becoming our First Place Winner is, 'Santas Airways Group'!"

As he called the name, the trophy came to light displaying the gold plate he'd had engraved with the winning name. There it was, elegantly inscribed saying exactly what he announced, 'Santas Airways Group'."

Telling the crowd, "If you will notice, I did not mention the creator of the First Place winner, since that person prefers to remain unknown. Because this name was unanimously voted into first place, I have to respect the winner's decision."

Looking at one another after this exposure, the stunned crowd took a little time to begin clapping in approval, considering the creator's name was not announced.

Suggesting as Santa went on, "What we will do is, to keep this trophy on display at the post office as a reminder of the unselfish people we encounter living in Santa Land!"

Margaret once again, pecking Santa's cheek with a kiss of approval, allowed the crowd to be drawn into an applauding mood.

Looking at Margaret, Santa said, "Thank you Sweetheart . . . as he returned the kiss, "but you know what I need?"

Margaret asked, "And what is that my Love?"

Answering her discreetly, Santa uttered, "A nap Hon," and she led him off the stage, while inquiring if Alex had enough help to clean up the mess left on the grounds; as the area slowly grew quiet, everyone dispersed.

Margaret and Santa found their way to his office where she knew he would enjoy napping in his favorite chair. She told him that first she was going to her office and when he awoke, she would most likely have dinner ready.

Running into Dorothy and Mary enroute to her office, she invited them in for some girlish chatter.

Not knowing the name of the winner of the Naming Contest, Mary remarked, "Girls, what did you think of the name which was chosen as the winner in the Naming Contest?"

Playing dumb, because they were all present when it was chosen; but only two of them knew to whom the creation belonged. Margaret was not about to confess to, knowing the winner's name.

Nonchalantly, Dorothy playing the picture of innocence

commented, "And what about that trophy inscribed with 'Donor Anonymous'; that must have taken a whole lot of restraint to refuse a first place trophy by someone so talented as to come up with the chosen name."

Only Margaret knew, in reality Dorothy was patting herself on the back.

Wanting to change the subject, Margaret inquired about holding their very own meeting and Mary responded, "Don't make it too soon . . . I can use the time the men and children are gone to take a good rest . . . as a matter of fact . . . when are the men returning to Ireland?"

Answering Mary's question Dorothy suggested, "The children have to be back in school, so I imagine it will be in the next few days. Fred hasn't mentioned anything regarding packing his clothes, but I suppose he'll do that when he comes in from cleaning the grounds.

"Likewise, I suppose Donald will do the same," added Mary.

Surmising Santa was asleep in his office, Margaret insisted they should all be on their way home before the men arrived and Dorothy and Mary found no problem with that suggestion.

Before returning to the kitchen, Margaret set out for Santa's office to see if he was still asleep. Entering the room, Margaret found him wide awake sitting in his chair thinking over the accomplishments of the day. Inviting her to take a seat she did so, patiently wondering what he had in mind..

"Margaret, I have a new project to engage when we go back in July to put Santa Claus on that trial basis," he revealed.

Asking what that might be, Margaret continued to listen to

Santa's Second Chance

Santa's declaration.

"Tell me," he said, "what did you think of the Talent Show?"

Not expecting this question, Margaret did not immediately respond, and Santa continued, "I for one was very impressed. As a matter of fact, I was so affected, I'm giving some thought to taking them with me when we return in July. However, I'll need your help with costumes; Fred and Donald will have to sell the idea to Mr. Tankeroo. Maybe, when we go back on our next trip . . ."

At this point Margaret interrupted saying, "You know this trip will have to be in the next few days, don't you?"

Responding positively, Santa announced, "Well that's all-right, I'll explain to Donald and Fred what I have in mind and ask them if they think they can sell it to Mr. Tankeroo. I doubt that they will have any objections; they did so well, selling him the idea of Santa Claus in July!"

Being in awe of Santa's thoughts, Margaret admitted she liked the idea and added, "Maybe while you are gone, I can take the subject up with Mary and Dorothy and I imagine they'll love helping to design and sew costumes for them!"

Santa then explained, "But I really should talk to Alex about this first; not only to see if he thinks it doable, but also to get the performers approval."

Santa was anxious to discuss the matter with Alex, but because Margaret told him dinner would soon be ready, Santa put it off till the next day; "All this thinking for one day," as he told Margaret ". . . is taxing my brain!"

Though they were enjoying their spring vacation, the children were anxiously awaiting their return to school.

Looking forward to spending time in Ireland, where he had not been for some time, Alex planned on visiting friends who stayed behind when he first moved to Santa Land. There was no way of telling if they were still around, some of them may have relocated. Of course, Leon and Phillip along with Nancy and Mildred would be there, so even without his friends he would still have his comrades, as well as Santa, Fred and Donald.

Days before they were to leave for Ireland, Santa summoned Alex to his office and his arrival was prompt.

"I wonder what kind of undertaking Santa is dreaming up now," Alex asked himself.

Once in his office, Santa greeted him with an air of gaiety and Alex with his usual inquiry asked, "What's up my friend?" as he sat at the desk in the special chair Santa had designed for him. It was made to be pumped up, thus propelling Alex to reach a comfortable level equivalent to Santa.

Continuing with a review of the Talent Show, Santa tried to question Alex about the individual performers, but not being able to explain exactly what it was he really wanted to know, regarding their capabilities, he went on to tell Alex how impressed he was with their performance.

Listening carefully and adjusting his memory by setting it into reverse mode, Alex seemed to recall Santa, at a previous meeting, mentioning something about talented performers in an exhibition. His perception was about to draw a vision of what he thought Santa was trying to promote! "Santa," Alex asked, "is a traveling talent group what you have in mind?"

Quickly blurting out, "Yes . . . that's exactly what I was thinking; how clever of you to read my mind."

Santa's Second Chance

Santa then added, "My question of course is . . ., do you think your comrades would be willing to put their wonderful talents on display?" Once again, relaying to him how impressed he was with their performances, Santa concluded, "Why Alex, they have talents that should be exposed to the world. And once again, I want to make this happen; you know, just like I helped the Angel Marion deliver her gifts to Mary, Joseph and the Baby Jesus, I still haven't forgotten."

Tilting his head, Alex answered, I would have to discuss this with them . . . and you want all seven of them?" and Santa said, "Yes, all seven.

Margaret said she would help design their costumes and she thought Mary and Dorothy would contribute their expertise. If you had seen what Margaret made to cover their ears when we went to the circus, you'd know we could do it. They could be called, 'THE ENTERTAINING ELVESTOS'.

What I had in mind was having them entertain at the Toy Thrillers Store in July, when I play Santa Claus; but only on a trial basis. If it works, we'll go from there. If it doesn't, we'll drop the whole idea, fair enough?"

Answering Santa with, "Fair enough," Alex said, "I'll discuss it with them and let you know." He left the office with Santa in a state of exuberance.

Checking with Margaret to see if she had him packed to leave in the next few days, he found everything in order.

Asking him about his meeting with Alex, Santa described it as successful . . . he felt certain, as entertainers they would agree to his plan. All they needed would be for Dorothy and Mary to help Margaret work on the costumes she would design.

Asking Santa if it was okay to mention the project to them,

he could see no reason to hide the expectation of success when it came to their new organization.

With the next question, Margaret inquired, "Do Fred and Donald know they are going to have to sell this program to Mr. Tankeroo?" Answering her, Santa explained, "Hon, if Fred and Donald sold him our Santa's program in the first place, he will no doubt agree as we will tell him this is a part of the original idea. And let's face it, this is nothing but excess publicity for his store, and why would he say no?

When we get back to Ireland, I'll have Donald and Fred pay him a visit so he can get an idea of what we'll need to make this event special. As for Mary and Dorothy, I think you had better hold off telling them till after we've returned from Ireland and I'll tell Fred and Donald when we get there.

Besides, I need Alex's okay to go ahead since he's the one who will be introducing the idea to them, and with the talent possessed by these seven, why would they refuse?

There's only one thing you will have to keep in mind when designing their costumes. Their ears will have to be covered so they will be recognized as little people, or even children."

Excitedly Santa murmured, "Margaret, this is going to be a real extravaganza; and I can hardly wait to play Santa, as well as to introduce . . .

THE ENTERTAINING ELVESTOS"

"NO CHARGE"

Having several thoughts she wanted to discuss with Santa, Margaret changed the topic of conversation to Snapper and Mitzi.

"Have you noticed how fond of Mitzi Snapper seems to be?" she asked, and went on saying, "I wonder who is missing this sweet dog?" and then surprisingly Margaret asked, "Do you suppose we should take her back with us, just in case someone puts in a claim for her at the pound . . . ?"

Santa quickly blurted out, "Take her back . . . and break Snapper's heart! You've got to be kidding Margaret."

Questioning Santa's response, she asked . . . "Snapper's heart or your heart?"

Defending his comment Santa remarked, "Well if it's my heart it's also your heart."

"If we don't find her owner, at least we should take her back to have her spayed, and since I'm not going along, maybe you can have this taken care of," advised Margaret.

Thinking about this proposal Santa suggested, "Maybe it would be a good idea for you to come along Hon. You could take care of Mitzi and I'll handle the other chores."

"And what will I tell Mary and Dorothy when they find out I'm going to make the trip, they too will want to come along," commented Margaret.

"They may notice your absence but if we don't tell anyone, they won't be able to observe it until after we've departed," stated Santa.

Following up with, "Well . . . I imagine a little underhandedness won't hurt considering the source to which it is being directed. Besides, it was Mary who said she needed a rest, so I might as well tell them I took her literally when we return home from Ireland."

"Good thinking," uttered Santa. Again with a vote of confidence, he added, "Margaret I really enjoy having your company on these trips, so pack your bags Hon, we're off to Ireland."

"When are we leaving," she inquired and Santa answered, 'Weather Permitting', possibly tomorrow, early A.M."

Showing a gesture of surprise, Margaret announced, "I'd better start packing," and Santa agreed. At the same time he said, "I'll check with Alfred to see what kind of weather we are going to have."

Finding him leaving the post office and on his way to the weather tower Santa called and asked, "How's the weather doing Alfred?"

Answering Santa with certainty, he described the next week as a traveler's dream. He detailed the weather as being brisk over head, but as one travels southwest, warm for at least the next week. Beyond then, he couldn't vouch for accuracy since weather in the springtime was so unpredictable.

Knowing he needed extra help, Santa invited him to come along. This would allow Santa a two-fold purpose; help while in Ireland as well as a weather interpretor for the return trip.

Asking Alfred if he knew where he might find Alex, he suggested Santa try the workshop, and this he did. "Where else would I expect to find him?" Santa said to himself. As luck would have it, Santa was coming through the door as Alex was coming out.

"Well, that was easy," commented Santa to Alex as they ran into one another.

Expressing his news with an overwhelming enthusiasm he told Alex of his decision to invite Alfred and that Margaret would also be coming along. At the same time, he asked him not to mention her attendance to anyone. "Also Alex," he said, "we will probably need the large sleigh and the cart. Margaret is taking Mitzi along to be spayed. The children of course can travel in the cart along with Mildred, Nancy, Leon and Phillip, and don't forget Alfred; Donald, Fred, Margaret with Mitzi, you and I will be traveling in the sleigh. Maybe we won't need the large sleigh. Alfred reports the weather will be good for the whole week.

By the way," continued Santa, "are 'THE ENTERTAINING ELVESTOS' going to perform for us?"

"Oh yes," I was going to tell you . . ." replied Alex.

Expecting a negative answer and not being able to wait for the confirmation Santa anxiously asked, "Are you sure they won't come along?"

Appearing puzzled and confused Alex asked, "You mean they are to come along . . . on this trip . . .?"

Realizing his error, Santa said, "No, I'm sorry Alex, I meant in July and Alex replied, "That's better . . . for a moment I thought you were talking about now.

Anyway, after careful consideration of the few problems involved, their answer was . . . 'Yes'! They would love to do some entertaining, just say the word and they will be ready."

Being assured that Alex would get the word out to all about going on the early A.M. trip, Santa bid him, "Goodnight!"

Santa and Margaret went to sleep extra early so arising for the A.M. trip wouldn't be a problem. The biggest problem for Santa would probably be, having to leave enjoyable dreams behind and consequently, losing a night of entertainment.

Awakening at an early hour, everyone found their way to the sleigh; the time to leave was at hand. Jake had fastened the cart where it should be in advance so when Fred and Donald arrived with the children, they automatically crawled in where they could be comfortable with Leon, Phillip, Nancy and Mildred.

Alex and Alfred rode with Santa and Margaret to be able to assist with Mitzi who was also riding in the sleigh.

Taking their places, Fred and Donald heard Santa bellow, "Is everyone secure and ready?" When he saw nothing but affirmative, shaking heads and smiles Santa called to his patiently waiting reindeer, "Let's GO GUYS!" and they were on their way.

The stars were out in number and the night sky was awesome. The ride was smoother than smooth and in what seemed like record time, it was over!

When they arrived in Ireland, all scurried into the house and looked forward to a hearty breakfast prepared by Mildred and Margaret. They soon came to be known as Mildred and Margaret, 'THE M & M TEAM'.

Suggesting they take short naps if necessary, Santa announced he would hold a meeting in the afternoon and he would like the attendance of all present.

While everyone who chose to nap did so, he and Margaret

decided their next step would be to the vet's office with Mitzi in anticipation of her oncoming operation.

Deciding it was a bit early, as the vet's office might not yet be open, Margaret suggested Santa draw up plans for his approaching engagement.

Sitting down to make notes on just what was needed and what he'd have to do, he began with his dress; that part was easy since he was using a red suit like the one Margaret had sewn for him when they married; but then he said to Margaret, "Hon, there seems to be something missing!"

Answering him with a profound thought she concluded, "Maybe you need a hat; coming from the North Pole, you should have something covering your head, and also . . . big black boots like those you would wear to trudge through the snow, and . . . considering the time of year, we might even find some great sales on them; after all, why would anyone wear boots in this season?"

Answering her suggestion, he said, "Good thinking, Margaret. That takes care of problem No. One.

Now, for Problem No. Two: We'll have to talk to Fred and Donald about selling the entertainment value of 'THE ENTERTAINING ELVESTOS' to Mr. Tankeroo.

Problem No. Three: We'll need a chair in which a Santa can sit; Fred and Donald will also have to discuss this with Mr. Tankeroo so he will have sufficient time to find one!

Problem No. Four: We will draw up the advertising but Mr. Tankeroo, having to place it in the newspapers will have to give us a deadline date enabling us to get the advertising to him in due time.

Margaret," Santa asked, "Are you writing these problems on paper? You know I'm not too good about being able to remember all of the details?" and she assured him she was.

Continuing with Problem No. Five: Santa said, "It seems to me as if we will need a bullhorn and a platform on which the entertainers can stand.

Then we have Problem No. Six: We will also need a cordoned off area in which people can line up with their children as they wait to visit with Santa.

Now," he went on, "to entice the public, we could have a grab bag. I might add, for this occasion only, we will give a gift to each child who visits with Santa. In the future, this will be up to the toy store, as to whether or not they wish to employ a tactic of this sort!

As I said, for this occasion only, we will supply the gifts and toys Margaret; we have so many in storage."

Margaret then asked, "But how will you know how many gifts to bring?"

With this question, Santa suggested, "How about if we make this offer to the public in our advertising and give them to the first twenty-five people in line. We certainly have an over abundance of items in our storeroom; at least twenty-five we could give away as gifts, and just think of the good will it would produce."

"That is an outstanding idea Santa," remarked Margaret. "There is no doubt in my mind that this whole strategy is going to be successful;" then she asked, "How many more problems do we have Hon?"

Answering he stated, "We'll have to think of Problem No.

Santa's Second Chance

Seven, as a question and answer project. This will be a daunting experience and to be honest with you, how does one answer an intimidating question?"

With seriousness in her voice, she softly mouthed the words, "Very carefully!"

Then he asked, "And what about the men who are going to play Santas; will they know how to handle this situation?"

Wisely Margaret advised, "We will have to wait and see; remember," she added, "one step at a time."

"Speaking of one step at a time," Santa asked, "Don't you think we should be on our way to the vet's office with Mitzi?"

"Yes," agreed Margaret, "but first we will have to stop at the pound to see if anyone has put in a claim for her!" Finding no results at the pound, they went on their way.

Reaching their destination, they were informed that the Spay and Neuter Clinic was held the next day. The technician at the veterinarian's office told them the doctor was out to lunch, but if they wanted to leave Mitzi, they could pick her up tomorrow. Completing the necessary papers giving their consent they returned home.

It wasn't long before the meeting time Santa had announced was to begin; even though they missed lunch, he still believed in promptness.

Calling the meeting to order, Santa asked Nancy if she was ready to take notes for the first meeting of 'Santas Airways Group'. Assuring him she was ready, he continued.

"First on my list is our effort to make Santa Claus a real, living person, whom we expect to last for possibly, decades. Obstacles must be overcome to make this happen; not only in the eyes of those involved but for those wanting a better life, for their children . . . and their children . . . etc., etc., etc . . . sort of like everlasting, endlessness. Before this can be accomplished, there are a lot of details to be worked out, so here goes!

Fred and Donald, you did a great job in selling Mr. Tankeroo our Santa Clause's trial program. However, I've come up with an addition to the event."

Beaming with recognition, Fred and Donald sat listening to Santa describe his plan. Continuing with his explanation, he reminded them of the Talent Show held at the Festival and the seven performers who tied for first place. "Being impressed with their performance," Santa went on, "I have decided to make them a feature of the Santas Airways Group as the 'ENTERTAINING ELVESTOS'. Their entertainment should bring in more people and Margaret is designing costumes for them so there should be no question about their origin.

Their talent is unquestionable, and it will be your job to sell the program to Mr. Tankeroo as a part of our Santa Claus program, called, 'CHRISTMAS IN JULY'."

At first Fred and Donald looking at one another seemed upset, thinking, what more does Santa want? Quickly reconsidering their misunderstanding, Fred thought that's a wonderful addition! Why not . . . whatever it takes and it was then Fred realized he and Donald were totally committed to Santa's project. With very little convincing, they agreed to finish selling the program to Mr. Tankeroo!

Santa complimented their efforts, knowing he needed complacence, not disagreement.

After all, Fred was thinking to himself, we've already sold one program, what's the difference if we just tell Mr. Tankeroo we've added something that will compliment the original plan, so Fred and Donald agreed to go along with Santa's idea.

Presenting them with the details of what he needed for the balance of the program, Santa could foresee little problem with his plan.

Not wanting to tell of obstacles which did not involve this crew Santa said, "We do have several other issues to cover and one of them . . . well no . . . actually the only other hindrance will be with the advertising for the Christmas in July program. Fred you will have to talk to Mr. Tankeroo so Leon and Phillip will know what type and size of advertising to draw up; also get a due date for the advertising to be placed in the local news.

You will have to tell him Santa needs a chair, a platform for the entertainers, along with an area to be cordoned-off where people will wait with the children wanting to visit Santa.

Does anyone have any recommendations, comments, helpful hints, anything that can or might improve our program?"

Raising his hand Alex directed his comment to Fred and Donald telling them, "By making the needed platform back in Santa Land, it could be brought with us when we return in July. In this way the stress of having to find one could be eliminated. If you can get the measurements, we can make it; all he will need to find is an empty space in which to place it. You two can get this point across when you iron out the details with him. As a matter of fact, Mr. Tankeroo would probably feel more agreeable toward these performers if it were less work for him!"

Knowing this idea came from Alex, Santa did not hesitate to approve it since he could picture the stage being put together in the workshop.

Fred and Donald discussed it being easier to sell if Mr. Tankeroo could see the entertainment value, and so the matter was settled!

The next step was getting Fred and Donald off to consult Mr. Tankeroo thus obtaining a go-ahead response so they could rush back to Santa Land to prepare for the trip back to Ireland to play out, 'CHRISTMAS IN JULY'."

While Fred and Donald prepared on the next day to contact Mr. Tankeroo, Santa and Margaret discussed rescuing Mitzi from the veterinarian's office.

Everyone arose to an early morning wake-up call, a great breakfast and the children returning to school.

Fred and Donald started right out to the Toy Thrillers Store as Santa and Margaret picked an appropriate time to retrieve Mitzi.

Since they were possibly going to return to Santa Land the next morning Santa and Margaret went grocery shopping. They purchased groceries to fill the bare cupboards in the house, as well as, enough to fill the emptying pantries in Santa Land.

Fred and Donald had returned in time for lunch and both were happy to give Santa the good news. Mr. Tankeroo had totally accepted their proposal and this made Santa a very happy trouper.

The day flew and after lunch Santa and Margaret decided enough time had passed to start out for the vet's office.

Reaching his office they were taken to a private room. As they sat down to wait for the attendant to deliver Mitzi, the doctor came in. Introducing himself as Dr. Dilly, Santa and Margaret returned the formality.

Being the first to speak, Dr. Dilly said, "Mr. and Mrs. Klaus,

Santa's Second Chance

I'm sorry I was out to lunch when you arrived yesterday, otherwise I would have told you . . ."

Because he faltered, Margaret suspiciously asked the doctor if something was wrong . . . ?

Smiling while answering, "No . . . no . . . not at all!" and hesitating again, he finally went on, "Not if you love your dog!"

Looking puzzled, Margaret again, with greater strength inquired, "Is something wrong doctor?"

His direct reply insinuated, "There is a problem of sorts, but nothing that time won't take care of."

Thinking of Snapper, Santa just listened as Margaret and the doctor concluded that he was unable to perform this operation because Mitzi was going to have puppies in the not too distant future.

Margaret was aghast. Being equally surprised, Santa took the news in his stride.

The attendant delivered Mitzi ready to return home as the doctor told Margaret, for the operation he didn't do, there was . . .

"NO CHARGE"

,

SANTA CLAUS COMES TO TOWN

With the entire group having made a final trip to Ireland, ready for the trial performance, Santa decided one more meeting to line up their objectives would be in order. Needing a chance to get their wits about them, he thought they should have an opportunity to acclimate themselves to their surroundings.

Since there wasn't enough sleeping room for everyone in the house, Santa asked Fred and Donald to come out to the barn with him as he needed to do some rearranging, and their help would be appreciated.

"Let me see," commented Santa. "We have seven performers. Then we have Alfred, Alfonso, Punky and Alex, plus Mildred, Phillip, Leon and Nancy. If Mildred and Nancy share their room with Sheila, Holly, Jessica and Meagan, we will have sufficient room out here for the rest of the crew."

Fred and Donald along with Santa started rearranging hay when Fred said, "I've got an idea . . . maybe several of them can sleep in the sleigh. Dorothy and I can sleep on the sofa and Donald and Mary can use one bed while you and Margaret use the other bed. This time, the children can sleep on the floor."

The first night looked like wall-to-wall people, but they did what they had to do.

Checking with Phillip and Leon to see how the advertising was coming along, Phillip showed Santa copies of what would appear in the newspapers one week before their extravaganza began. It read:

COME ONE . . . COME ALL . . . TO OUR FIRST

CHRISTMAS IN JULY ! ! ! !

BRING YOUR CHILDREN TO MEET A REAL GIFT-
GIVING SANTA CLAUS OFFERING A FREE GIFT TO THE
FIRST 25 CHILDREN ! ! !

* * * * * * *

PERFORMING DURING SANTA'S VISIT

WILL BE

THE ENTERTAINING ELVESTOS

ONE DAY ONLY ON JULY FOURTH ! ! !

This advertising would appear in the newspaper for one straight week or seven days before the beginning of July.

Hurrying to the Toy Thrillers Store to check on some of the details with Mr. Tankeroo, Fred and Donald were to make certain enough space had been cleared on the floor to allow the stage they were bringing in to be properly positioned. He was cooperative and agreeable about everything they suggested; and also showed them the chair he found resembling a throne in which Santa could sit as he received the children.

When Fred and Donald reported the outcome of their visit to Santa, he was complimentary about their course of action, which seemed destined to become a fantastic success.

Santa approached Margaret regarding the black boots he needed to wear with his red suit and the hat she would design and put together. Suggesting the same store she recommended to Donald and Fred when they were looking for shoes, she and

Santa went looking for boots.

The minute they walked through the door, he spotted the black boots he needed and crossed his fingers hoping they were his size. Sure enough they were, so he and Margaret paid for the boots and exited the store as quickly as they could for fear someone might be looking for the same boots.

The day for which Santa waited was finally at hand; the stage had been set in place and the advertisement in the newspaper looked well positioned. Santa at last found himself dressed as the Santa Claus he imagined Santa to be.

Working his way through throngs of people waiting outside the store, Mr. Tankeroo opened the front door to allow his guests of honor to come in. He showed Santa the chair he had prepared for him and the stool sitting next to it, should a child need to sit down.

After all, the line beginning to form grew quite long and Mr. Tankeroo was uncertain about Santa's age, and whether or not he could handle the children on his knees; hence, waiting could be tiresome, leaving the children with a need to sit once they ended up at his chair.

Santa brought along the 'ENTERTAINING ELVESTOS' but saw to it they entered through a back door so they wouldn't be mobbed by the gathering crowd.

Having come dressed in their costumes, after bringing them inside, Mr. Tankeroo provided a private room where they could wait until it was time after for the them to perform.

Fred and Donald were also available to help with whatever needed to be taken care of.

The crowd seemed to be eagerly enthralled, and then Santa

accompanied by Fred and Donald made his appearance on the makeshift stage.

Margaret watched from behind the scenes; she knew if anything went wrong, she wanted to be there for Santa should he need help.

Donald called the crowd to order and Fred asked them to fall in line with their children at the cordoned off area.

Taking over the pleasure of introductions, Donald said to the crowd, "My friends! I want to welcome you all to the first, but certainly not the last visit to be held by Santa Claus; however, not regularly in July. We are simply checking to see if this arrangement can be presented with joyous endeavor at the time of year better known as Christmas.

We all know that giving comes from the heart, but can we open our hearts enough to duplicate this occurrence? We feel as if you can, given the desire along with a little help year after year, from one better known as Santa Claus? Today, Santa is here to help establish this pattern and what better way to grow than to start with the children.

If you will line up, Santa will be answering their questions, and they will be telling him what it is they would like to receive as a Christmas gift. When you hear the conversation between them, you can make of it what you will. This year we are making an exception because at this time, we are doing a dress rehearsal, six months early.

Do notice," Donald continued, "Mr. Tankeroo, the manager of this store has decorated it gorgeously with ornaments to help put you in a Christmas mood.

In the future, this will only happen in the weeks before Christmas to assist those of you who celebrate in December . . .

on the twenty-fifth to be exact, the birthday of Jesus Christ."

Then Donald added, "Oh, I almost forgot . . . while the children are waiting to visit with Santa Claus, we have some entertainment for you, namely the 'ENTERTAINING ELVESTOS' straight from Santa Land.

Donald called Holly as their first entertainer and she tap danced and sang to the tune of 'A HAPPY PLACE' as the children began their encounters with Santa.

His first visitor was a little girl named Lorene. When Santa asked if she had been a good girl . . . she sharply answered, "I have probably been a better girl than you have been a good boy!"

Telling him she wanted a toy railroad train, he asked if her parents knew this and disappointedly, she replied, "Yes, but they think I should have a doll."

Misunderstanding her answer, Santa handed her a doll he had pulled from his bag filled with gifts. Seeing it, she responded, "Oh good, now I have a doll, so maybe my parents will finally get me a toy train!"

Watching her go on her way, Santa feeling flabbergasted waited for the next child approaching his chair. This child was on crutches so it took a few moments for him to get there.

Asking this little boy, who told Santa his name was Andre', what kind of gift he would like to receive, he explained, in very little detail, and to Santa's surprise, "Sir . . . , if you can find a pair of braces that would fit my broken legs . . . then I'll be able to throw these crutches away, and maybe, if you could . . . , include a bat and ball so I can play baseball with the other boys."

Knowing he couldn't ask this child if he'd been good . . ., in

Santa's Second Chance

Santa's mind how could he be bad . . ., then told him, "Andre'. I'll put in a special order for those braces and meanwhile, would you like this book to read while you are waiting for them to be delivered?" Oddly, as Andre' took the book, he murmured, "Thank you," and "GOD BLESS YOU!" Being truly amazed, Santa wiped a tear from his eye.

It was time for another performer and Fred introduced Sheila singing 'ALWAYS NEAR'.

The crowd without a doubt was enjoying the entertainment, and the line of children moved quickly with Santa asking and answering as many questions as he could.

As the twenty-sixth child approached Santa's chair, with all the free gifts gone, a little girl named Judy, when questioned if she'd been a good girl, quite boisterously asked him, "Does it make any difference? I'm not going to get a free gift; why didn't you bring more of those prizes?"

Not knowing what to tell her, Santa said, "I think you are right, so next time I will find a few more, but for now, I'll tell you what! How about if I give you a rain check?"

Knowing what a rain check was, Judy answered, "Okay!" After giving Santa her request he summoned Fred to accompany Judy, to a counter where he found someone who could help with a rain check.

When he returned to the stage, it was time to introduce Frank for some crooning magic with an old song called, 'MEM'RY'." He sang it so beautifully, he almost brought more tears to Santa's eyes.

By this time, with food in mind, Santa was heard saying, "It must be lunchtime." Beckoning Fred, Santa told him he needed some lunch and would he arrange this with Mr. Tankeroo.

Mr. Tankeroo, was also hungry and had the thoughtfulness to have a luncheon prepared and waiting for all the involved participants in a back room. They found him overjoyed since the cash register had been ringing wildly all morning, just as if it were . . . . . Christmas.

After everyone finished lunch, they resumed their places and in no time at all, Santa's line of visiting children were again responding to his questions, and he to theirs.

Time was passing, and the store personnel began to close its doors for the evening. There was little doubt about this project being a total success.

Santa felt bad about the children he was unable to talk with, there seemed to be so many; but then, Fred felt an attack of inspiration, and he had a vision of what he thought could be an admirable solution.

Once they were home enjoying the delicious meal Mildred had cooked, they chatted among themselves and Fred, upon finding an opportune moment, questioned Santa with, "You know the children you were unable to talk to because you ran out of time?"

Santa listened as Fred went on, "What do you think about the idea of leaving an address where they could write you in Santa Land, thus enabling them to make their wishes known; you know, like Jessica and Bronson sang in their duet, 'WISHING'?"

Joining in with Fred's statement Donald added, "All we would have to do is leave a sign at the toy store or perhaps even put a short notice in the newspaper like: If you missed your chance to talk to Santa, you can write to:

Santa's Second Chance

SANTA CLAUS

℅ Santa Land

North Pole

Send your letter to the address listed above.

Santa may not be able to answer everyone directly . . . however, if you write your name and return address on a stamped envelope he will receive your letter.

Santa thought this was a magnificent plan and while thinking of the idea as an outstanding choice, he added, "At this time, I also want to congratulate our 'ENTERTAINING ELLVESTOS' for a wonderful performance; I never realized we had such accomplished talent in our village."

Going on to one more important matter, Santa asked Donald and Fred to visit The Toy Thrillers Store to get some feedback from Mr. Tankeroo before they returned to Santa Land.

Thinking that was a good idea, they all felt an air of fatigue, wearying not only their bodies but minds as well.

Everyone helped with the dishes as well as straightening the house and before long, they all went to bed ready to fall into a conscientious night of sleep so they could wake early in the morning to begin the completion of a new program called . . . .

SANTA CLAUS COMES TO TOWN

Irene Zulueta

THE NEXT PURSUIT

With the first item on the agenda for the next day being the trip to the Toy Thrillers Store to check feedback from Mr. Tankeroo, Fred and Donald dressed once again as the successful salesmen they were becoming. Starting out early in the morning they found themselves at the door as the store opened.

Welcoming the men Mr. Tankeroo exclaimed, "Come in, come in; I'm so happy to see you," and led them straight to his office.

Taking seats at his desk, they watched Mr. Tankeroo as he took out a check book and start preparing to write the men a check.

Speaking up, Fred inquired, "What are you doing?"

Explaining his position, Mr. Tankeroo told them, "Why I'm giving back."

Being dumbfounded, Donald asked, "Giving back . . . giving back what?"

Setting his pen back on the desk, he explained while asking at the same time, "Santa did such a great job, don't you think it's only fair to pay him for his time?"

"That sounds great," said Fred, "but Santa definitely said he would not charge you . . . so why would you write him a check?" Having a hard time accepting Santa's actions at 'NO CHARGE' Mr. Tankeroo felt bewildered.

Santa's Second Chance

After a bit of yes . . . no . . . yes . . . no . . ., Donald finally agreed but only if they were to ask Santa first, what he felt his charge would be.

Feeling these terms were acceptable, Mr. Tankeroo finally put his checkbook back in his desk drawer.

At this point, Fred and Donald tried to tell him exactly why they were there. Fred went on trying to obtain information from Mr.Tankeroo, while he, understanding what kind of info they were looking for took a firm stand and asked them to STOP . . . right where they were, and he would draw them a mental picture. The drawing was quite substantial.

"To begin with, said" Mr. Tankeroo, "Let's start with my cashier-secretary. I want to apologize for her negative outlook; but you see, she has been working, well . . . almost free for some time. When she saw the amount of sales rung up that day, she couldn't apologize hard enough for what she calls her despicable attitude.

We would definitely like to have Santa come back here at Christmas time and once again, we will be glad to pay him for his services."

While quietly listening as well as debating this proposition, Donald spoke up and commented, "Mr. Tankeroo, quite frankly, we know for a fact that Santa has other responsibilities and whether or not he can fulfill an obligation of this nature is a question only he can answer. Tell me," Donald went on, "just supposing Santa can't make it; if we substituted someone . . . let's say a look-a-like Santa. . . . would this be satisfactory?"

Thinking out loud, Mr. Tankeroo inquired, "Would he have the same demeanor . . . behavior . . . poise? And how about the 'ENTERTAINING ELVESTOS'," he asked. "Would they also perform for us?"

Fred and Donald looked at one another . . . they knew they could replace Santa, but in no way could they replace the ELVESTOS, nor did they think Santa would want to replace them. However, in his mind . . . Fred had another substantial thought and maybe he would mention it merely as an idea, to Santa when they provide him with the feedback. They made no promise and only said, "That's a possibility." Trying to revert to the original picture, Mr. Tankeroo told them, "The crowds we had in the store that day were beyond count; the sales I could never have believed . . . and to top it all . . ., in July!

Could you ever imagine people buying ornaments and decorations in July? Why . . . I'll have to place another huge order just to have them back in the store by Christmas; and at least . . . this time I'll have the money to pay for them in advance."

After telling Mr. Tankeroo about his latest aspiration, namely for children to write letters to Santa, if he allowed them to put a sign in his window with instructions on how to do it, Mr. Tankeroo came up with what he thought might be an even better idea.

The children could send their letters to the store. He in turn would have his secretary sort them out and parents could pick up the items when they were advertised on sale and whatever he did not carry in the store, he would order from Santa Land's toy supply and in this way both sides would profit.

"Outstanding," said Fred to Donald as their eyes widened to allow pictures of money floating from one eye to another throughout the atmosphere.

Then Mr. Tankeroo surprisingly asked, "But tell me . . . are

Santa's Second Chance

you going to offer this program to my competitors?"

Donald's and Fred's mouths dropped when they heard this question and it was Donald who came up with, "Mr. Tankeroo, you will have to understand this is a business. Eventually, this idea will spread and if we don't take control and offer it to others, there will be those who decide they could start a business like this of their own and who knows what kind of schemes they may concoct?

At least you know, with us, we are forthright, honest . . . we will work with you . . . we have the ability to produce what you might need . . . why . . . I'll bet we could even produce the set of leg braces that little boy called Andre' asked for."

Hearing this last comment, upon thinking of the little boy, Mr. Tankeroo wiped a tear running from his eye. Fred and Donald were unaware that the little boy belonged to his daughter; but he never let on or said a word about the situation, he merely uttered, "I suppose you are right, besides at least I'll have a head start; since you probably won't have all the Santas you need by Christmas time."

Then Donald made a suggestion saying, "Look Mr. Tankeroo, supposing we bring you a Santa this year and that will give you the head start of a whole year before we begin soliciting your competitors. Does this sound fair enough?"

Mr. Tankeroo agreed and as they parted company, Fred explained that all they discussed was not only top secret, but subject to Santa's approval; and as they left the store, he said, "Mum's the word."

Donald and Fred were thrilled to no end as they discussed the program on the way back to the house.

Searching for Santa and finding him they asked if they could have a meeting with Leon, Phillip and Nancy in their office, telling Santa, "When they hear of the feedback from our successful promotion and just what we are planning, they might have suggestions, ideas and so on to incorporate in a proposal of possibly future promotions."

Once again, Santa could see the maturing attitude of the two men in their willingness to let others work and share their ideas, in the process of building a business. In his mind the work was based on trust.

Proceeding to the executive office, they found all three of them at work and as they entered, Phillip asked, "How did everything go Fred?"

Bubbling with excitement Fred blurted out the details to what they were planning as Santa and the rest listened.

Then Donald added, "Santa, we told Mr. Tankeroo we needed your approval and mum's the word regarding any future plans.

We also mentioned we would give him a head start by bringing back a look-a-like Santa next Christmas, if necessary.

Now, if you want to play Santa for the next Christmas, it's okay, but if you would rather send a look-a-like we have four months in which to find and train someone to take your place.

Whether you do it or a look-a-like does it, means we will have another year to refine our training, hire receptive men and set up our toy business . . . and sell the promotion; how does that sound for starters?"

"Amazingly enough," responded Santa, "I think you two men have hit the nail on the head.

I will commit to being in town again for Christmas this year, as I really enjoyed the children . . . their sometimes arrogant

and snide remarks, while offered openly; yet they were inno-
cent children with comments we consider as, 'coming from the
mouths of babes' . . ."

That's what we need to impress upon our first look-a-like; so
he'll realize he's not a simple hireling."

Adding to the conversations Fred told Santa, "Mr. Tankeroo
also asked about the 'ENTERTAINING ELVESTOS' and all
we told him was . . . that's a possibility.

To bring them back at Christmas is fine, but there's no way
we can sell their services to future promotions.

However," Fred went on, "How about if the kids, meaning
Jayne, Jean and Joan along with the boys get an act together
and perhaps, they can earn some income to provide for their
future."

Being open to all ideas which promoted income, Santa said,
"That's good to begin with Fred, and of course, that's a decision
we should leave up to the children.

As for now, Nancy did you take notes of our ideas and pro-
posals here today?" inquired Santa.

Her comical, immediate answer being, "You betcha, every
bit of it!" made Santa realize that he actually had the outline for
a plan of what was to come.

His next step was to find Margaret so he could convey to her
the good news.

That night at dinner, Santa announced to everyone that their
mission had been accomplished and he added, "Our next step
will be to set up our training program after we return to Santa
Land.

Tomorrow I will confer with Leon and Phillip regarding advertising for a look-a-like Santa Claus and we will return in November to begin our next pursuit.

Asking the ELVESTOS if they too would like to return, he found their enthusiasm heartwarming and set the final performance in motion by telling Fred and Donald to return to the Toy Thrillers Store to confirm with Mr. Tankeroo everything they discussed. Tell him I approved of everything and God willing, Santa will be back this year the same as he was in July with the 'ENTERTAINING ELVESTOS' and maybe even more giveaways.

With the meeting coming to an end, Donald mentioned one other subject on which they needed to concentrate.

When Fred asked him, "And what might that be?" Donald explained, "Do you remember telling Mr. Tankeroo that we could produce braces for that little boy called Andre'?"

Recollecting the conversation, Fred said, "Yes, I distinctly remember our telling him we could probably produce those braces in Santa Land . . . but it was only a figure of speech!"

Then Donald described a bigger picture of the problem as he mentioned, "Did you notice the tear that came to Mr. Tankeroo's eye when we discussed the situation?"

Answering, Fred concurred, "Well . . . sort of . . ."

Continuing, Donald explained, "My intuition tells me, he knows this boy and . . . "

Impatiently Fred said, "And what?"

Rather than deal with Fred's impatience Donald declared, "Let's just ask him if he can get the length of braces and how wide around they should be to fit the little boy. Punky would be able to make a set of braces for this fellow and everyone would be forever grateful."

There was still time in the day for Fred and Donald to return to the Toy Thrillers Store to confirm all of the stipulations they had discussed earlier which had already been given Santa's approval.

When Donald asked Mr. Tankeroo about the boy called Andre', he mentioned that the boy had been in earlier with his mother and they came to the store on a regular basis, but he still did not tell them the boy was his grandson.

Explaining his need for the information required, Donald also told him they would be leaving for home in several days.

Mr. Tankeroo felt certain he could gather this information quickly without exposing the origin of the source.

Asking if he could have the necessary information by the next day Mr. Tankeroo happily replied he could. With nothing more to discuss Fred and Donald told him they would return tomorrow as their time before returning to Santa Land was running short.

After explaining the necessary return visit to the toy store, Santa decided to wait several more days before returning home.

Summer was such a lovely time in Ireland, Santa and Margaret took the opportunity to completely enjoy their visit in one another's company, but the time to depart had come.

Fred and Donald retrieved the necessary information, the cart was packed, and everyone in the sleigh readied themselves to travel through the skies, as Santa called out, "Let's GO GUYS!"

Irene Zulueta

In no time at all, they arrived home, raving about their successful endeavor to all and anxious to begin . . .

THE NEXT PURSUIT

A HAPPY PLACE
There's a happy place called Santa Land,

Where people work and play.

They laugh and smile,

For all the while,

Their hearts are young and gay.

They found a new way of living,

How life can be about giving,

They toil and help one another,

In Santa Land, L.A.

U.S.A.

Their animals are big and small,

They're growing day by day,

They fly and roam,

Away from home,

An aura on display.

Their village seems to be glowing,

In a special sort of way.

Santa's Second Chance

Well, should you ever wonder,

See Santa Land L.A.

U.S.A.

They finally found a way to say,

That Santa's here to stay.

He'll check your list,

And bring your gifts,

Then hurry on his way,

He knows that children are waiting,

Forever and a day,

So, find your special haven,

In Santa Land, L.A.

U.S.A.

Copyright August, 2008

Irene Pichlik Zulueta

Irene Zulueta